Praise for K.A. Mitchell's
Bad Company

"As always, Mitchell's characterization is perfect."

~ *Dear Author*

"Ms. Mitchell drew me in with vivid details, spicy scenes, and characters that stole my heart. I get to step into a world much like my own with people I can relate to."

~ *Whipped Cream Reviews*

"I have always enjoyed K.A. Mitchell's books because of the characterizations, and she didn't disappoint in *Bad Company*. The emotions are open and raw and the characters are realistically drawn."

~ *Reviews by Jessewave*

"Ms. Mitchell singes the pages with the passion that sparks between Kellan and Nate. *Bad Company* is oh-so-good—don't miss this book!"

~ *Joyfully Reviewed*

Look for these titles by
K.A. Mitchell

Now Available:

Custom Ride
Hot Ticket
Diving in Deep
Regularly Scheduled Life
Collision Course
Chasing Smoke
An Improper Holiday
No Souvenirs
Not Knowing Jack

Fragments Series
Life, Over Easy

Bad in Baltimore Series
Bad Company
Bad Boyfriend

Print Anthologies
Midsummer Night's Steam: Temperature's Rising
To All a (Very Sexy) Good Night
Serving Love

Bad Company

K.A. Mitchell

SAMHAIN
PUBLISHING

Samhain Publishing, Ltd.
11821 Mason Montgomery Road, 4B
Cincinnati, OH 45249
www.samhainpublishing.com

Bad Company
Copyright © 2012 by K.A. Mitchell
Print ISBN: 978-1-60928-595-1
Digital ISBN: 978-1-60928-474-9

Editing by Sasha Knight
Cover by Angela Waters

First Samhain Publishing, Ltd. electronic publication: June 2011
First Samhain Publishing, Ltd. print publication: May 2012

Dedication

For Thomasine. Without peer pressure, there could be no Butterscotch Schnapps Book. Thanks for loving Kellan even when he was a jerk.

Thanks to Jennifer for the introduction to Baltimore, and thanks to Erin for keeping me company—*good* company.

Chapter One

Kellan licked dry lips before tugging open the door to J.J.'s bar. Stepping into the cool darkness after a long walk under Baltimore's late-spring sun had him blinking rapidly to keep from crashing into anything. Not that there was much to crash into. The bar was almost deserted.

He wasn't sure if that was a good thing. He'd never been in a gay bar before, and from the way they looked on TV and in the movies, he'd expected to be tripping over guys grinding away on each other. There wasn't anything wrong with that, but Kellan hoped he'd have time to work up to shirtless guy-on-guy grinding.

In addition to the absence of grinding, Kellan also noticed the lack of a disco ball and a thumping soundtrack. J.J.'s could have been any Baltimore bar at five thirty on a Monday afternoon, right down to ESPN playing on the set hanging over the bottles arranged behind the bartender.

The barstools weren't completely empty. As his eyes adjusted completely, Kellan saw what he'd come here for.

Kellan hadn't seen Nate Gray for fifteen years, but even with Nate's back to him, Kellan could have picked him out of a crowd much larger than the five guys in the bar. Who else would sit up that straight, especially on a barstool? Nate would never change. Kellan pictured the too-serious expression Nate always wore, lips tight like he was afraid to smile too much, dark anxious eyes behind those round Harry Potter glasses— which Nate had worn years before anyone knew who Harry Potter was.

Nate turned like he could feel Kellan's stare then quickly turned away. Had Nate recognized him? Even if Nate wasn't happy to see him—and given the way Kellan had acted back in ninth grade, he couldn't blame him—it didn't matter. The long walk had given Kellan more than dry lips and sun blindness. It had made him twice as goddamned sure he taught Geoffrey Brooks he couldn't control his son the way he ran his company.

That determination had Kellan striding down to the end of the bar to jostle Nate's elbow and blurt out, "Hey, Nate. So, you're still gay, right?"

Unfortunately, Kellan's timing sucked. Nate choked, spewing what he'd just drunk from the Corona bottle across Kellan's left sleeve. Kellan used the excuse of slapping him on the back to wipe off his arm.

Nate shook him off, wiped his own face with the back of his hand and turned. Kellan had been right. Nate didn't look very happy to see his old friend.

Well, maybe friend was pushing it after the way things had gone back then. But they'd been friends for seven years before that one year when they weren't. If Nate would let him, Kellan could make it up to him. The sneak attack might not have been the best idea, but it was getting late and unless Kellan wanted to spend the night on a park bench, he needed to get the ball rolling. Besides, once Nate heard the plan, Kellan knew he would go for it. Nate had almost as much reason to want to put the screws to old Geoffrey as Kellan did.

Nate's eyes, already uncomfortably different without the familiar glasses, were half-lidded and lazy as he took his time looking Kellan up and down, gaze lingering on Kellan's crotch long enough to make him squirm. "Kellan Brooks. My day from hell is complete. Yes. I'm still gay. And guess what?" Nate leaned in like he had a secret and then said in a loud whisper, "I think this is a gay bar. You might want to cover your ass with both hands as you run for the door. Wouldn't want to get any queer on you."

When this brilliant idea first hatched in Kellan's brain, he had skipped over the explaining-it-to-Nate part to get to picturing the look on the old man's face when he got the bad news.

Kellan could do this. Nate had always given in before. But it would be easier if he stopped sneering at Kellan as if he were dog shit stuck to Nate's shoe.

"Okay," Nate said, rolling his eyes after a long pause. "Now that we've cleared that up, I need another beer." He pushed the dripping bottle across the bar.

Kellan slid onto the barstool next to Nate. "I need a boyfriend."

Nate looked like he was going to start choking again, though his beer was empty, then his face went hard and still. "Blow me."

Kellan put a hand on Nate's sleeve, and Nate shook him off again. "You don't understand. I really need a boyfriend."

"No, you don't understand. I really need some head, so if you're not going to blow me, leave me the fuck alone." Nate shifted on his barstool, leaning forward and back, glancing over his shoulder. "I swear if someone from the paper is punking me—"

"Can I explain this to you?"

The bartender set a fresh beer in front of Nate.

"If you're paying, I'll listen." Nate nodded at the beer.

"I can't." Heat hit Kellan's cheeks, and he dropped his gaze.

"Right. You can't afford a beer." Nate slapped a ten on the bar and glanced around like someone would save him from having to deal with Kellan.

"I spent my last twenty on a cab to get to the paper. They said you'd be here, so I walked."

"A whole five blocks? Alert the media."

It had been more like fifteen. But with Nate sneering at him, showing the same kind of disgust Kellan's dad was always quick to dish out, the words died in his throat and the flush got hotter, spreading into his neck. His cheeks felt as lit up as Rudolph's famous nose. He'd never been able to stop it, but until now, Kellan thought he'd given up being ashamed. Funny that Nate could make him feel worse than the old man could. Even with what he'd thrown at Kellan today. He tried to catch Nate's gaze. "Will you listen to me?"

"Can you give me one single fucking reason why I should?"

With a desperate hope that Nate's memories went back a lot further than that year where things had gotten weird, Kellan shoved up his sleeve to show the scar on his forearm, knowing Nate had one to match, a gift from a spike on a cemetery fence to two seven-year-old boys who had snuck off late one night because Kellan had wanted to introduce his brother to his new friend. When they fell bleeding onto the ground outside the cemetery, Nate had suggested that they become brothers the way some kids had done in a book he read. Nate understanding how much Kellan missed having a big brother had been worth his mother's freakout and the terrifying tetanus shot when their adventure became public knowledge.

"That still count for anything?" Kellan pulled his sleeve back down.

"Didn't count for much as I remember." Nate's eyes narrowed, but there was nothing lazy about the look this time. "Cash, grass or ass, man."

"Huh?"

"Nothing's free. You won't blow me, you won't buy me a beer, and for damn sure I don't owe you any favors."

Kellan shrugged, trying for an ease he didn't feel. "Maybe you've got me confused with my dad, man, because I never did anything to you or your family."

"So that wasn't you laughing while your asshole friends showed the little faggot what a swirly was on the first day of high school?"

There wasn't anything Kellan could say to fix that. Couldn't explain why instead of sticking up for Nate the way he'd always done, this time Kellan had gone along, promising himself he was there to make sure things didn't get too carried away and that Nate didn't get hurt. Kellan knew that didn't count for much.

Nate slammed his beer onto the bar and stepped off the stool. "Well, this has been a fucked-up end to a long day. Good luck with that boyfriend thing. Play safe and remember to use lots of lube."

"Dude, wait."

Dude, man, Nate was sure there was a *bro* waiting somewhere behind lips that were a shade too full to go with the rest of Kellan's sharp features. Maybe the asshole really thought he could dump the blame on his dad then pretend it was just like the old days. Nate kept right on walking out of the bar.

He pulled his scooter off the sidewalk, strapped on his

helmet and turned the key. Kellan grabbed the handlebars.

Nate probably could have managed to take off without dragging seventy-five inches of Kellan Brooks across the sidewalk, but he snapped, "What?"

"I don't have anywhere to go."

What Nate meant to say was *Why the fuck is that my problem?* but what came out was "What do you mean?"

"My dad threw me out—cut me off—and..."

"What about your friends? Your fiancée?" Nate wanted to bite the words back and ended up biting his tongue. Now Kellan would know Nate had bothered reading up on the dickhead's life on the gossip sites, watched clips of him in that reality show he was on. In Nate's defense, he worked for a newspaper. There might have been a reason other than that he still gave a shit about the big idiot.

"We broke up," Kellan said flatly.

"Again? What was she, fiancée number five?" Damn, like that wasn't obviously bitter.

"Three." Kellan licked his lips.

Nate knew damn well Kellan wasn't flirting, sudden inexplicable quest for a boyfriend or not. But Nate didn't have a boyfriend, hadn't even had a hookup in over a month, and his eyes moved from the pink tongue on Kellan's lips to his green eyes and sun-streaked dirty-blond hair before Nate could remind himself that was a bad idea.

With a mental shake of his head, Nate said, "You've got to have some other friends. Because whatever I am, I'm not that anymore."

"I owe most of them money."

"Well, if you came looking for cash, you came to the wrong place."

The scooter between Nate's legs had suffered greatly in its previous existence as a vehicle of Chinese takeout. Despite the amount of non-wok oil and grease Nate had used to get it running again, the smell still hovered, unpleasant enough to cure him of a life-long craving for Kung Pao chicken.

Kellan still clung to the handlebars.

"Why did your dad throw you out?"

If Kellan said it was because he really had come out, Nate supposed he could find some sympathy in the midst of a big pile of serves-you-fucking-right. But the spark of sympathy drowned in a sudden stream of porn featuring Kellan's wide mouth panting and bruised from hard kisses sliding down Nate's cock, making him shift uncomfortably on the thin seat.

"Can I— Can we go someplace so I can explain it to you?"

Kellan didn't have the kind of big round eyes that should be necessary to pull off that wounded-puppy look. But it wouldn't be the first time that appeal had suckered Nate in. And his tendency to take in strays had convinced his parents Nate was destined to be a veterinarian.

He nodded.

Kellan let go of the handlebars.

"Are you going to hop on or jog alongside?" That sounded a lot more confident than the situation warranted. Nate wasn't exactly sure the scooter would make it ten blocks with Kellan's added weight.

Kellan swung a leg over from the back, the careful way he arranged himself a clear indication he was trying to limit his touch to scooter rather than anything made of Nate. That lasted until they lurched away from the curb and into rush-hour traffic. Kellan's hands landed first on Nate's shoulders, then on his hips.

As they stopped for a light on Eastern, Kellan leaned close, breath tickling Nate's ear. "What's that smell?"

Chapter Two

Kellan wasn't sure if the tiny bike had sputtered to death on this back street or if this was where Nate was taking them, but when Nate took off his helmet, Kellan eased himself off the back of the seat where he'd been trying to keep himself. He swore that when they'd zipped up Broadway, weaving in and out of traffic, Nate had been trying to dump him off.

Still without saying anything to him, Nate dragged the scooter up over the sidewalk and unlocked a green painted door. The street was only one car length wide, the buildings all squat squares of painted bricks with different color doors. Nate hauled the scooter through the door and put it next to a stairway that needed a fresh coat of baby-blue paint.

"Is this your house?"

Nate reached back out toward one of the three mailboxes next to the door. "It's my apartment."

Without a *this way* or *c'mon*, he started up the stairs. Without options, Kellan followed. Nate's apartment was bigger than Kellan expected from the outside. A good-sized living room held a couch and a desk. One wall made up the kitchen, with a counter separating it from the rest of the room.

Still without saying anything to Kellan, Nate put his keys on a hook near the door and walked over to drop his mail on the desk. Kellan hesitated next to the door, but when Nate took two beers out of the fridge and put them on the counter, the ache in Kellan's shoulders relaxed a little and he took the beer Nate held out.

There weren't any chairs, so they leaned, facing each other across the counter.

Nate took a long drink, though Kellan could feel Nate watch him around the neck of the bottle. Kellan drank a little of his, but the nerves multiplying like bunnies in his stomach weren't exactly interested in any liquid being dumped on them.

"So explain." Nate put his half-empty bottle on the counter.

Life should really have a fast-forward button so Kellan could get to the part where Nate was on his side without having to rehash all this shit in a way that didn't end up with Kellan wandering around Baltimore with seventy-five cents in his pocket and the clothes on his back.

A last-minute stay of execution arrived in a ball of gray fur leaping onto the counter. The cat sauntered between them, licked the lip of Nate's bottle and sat down to aim an appraising stare at Kellan.

"Quan Yin," Nate said, and Kellan assumed he was naming the cat and not starting a random discussion.

Kellan loved animals; Nate had too. There'd always been a few cats or a baby squirrel in need of nursing at the Grays' house. Kellan was more partial to dogs, wished he had one growing up, but after Keegan didn't come home from Kuwait, the Brooks' setter T-rex died of grief, and they never got another dog. Slicking his fingers with the condensation on his bottle, Kellan held them out toward the cat.

She sniffed then licked twice with a rough, tickling tongue. Kellan rubbed her chin and cheeks, and she purred enthusiastically, bumping his hand in encouragement.

Nate sighed.

"Animals like me," Kellan said in apology.

"I remember."

"That baby skunk you insisted we take to the vet? Remember?"

"You were the only one who could carry it without it spraying us."

"Yeah. Still had to take tomato-soup baths. Made my hair orange."

Nate's laugh turned into a quick, sharp cough.

Quan Yin managed to twine herself around his forearm, and Kellan kept rubbing and stroking. Her purr rivaled the engine on the scooter and probably had more power. Between the cat on his side and Nate's almost laugh, Kellan thought he might not end up in a homeless shelter.

"My father had some kind of meltdown after Delia and I broke up. I don't know what caused it." That wasn't completely true. His father had been apoplectic about the pictures that popped up in an online rag of Kellan with his face between the tits of some waitress in Miami.

Delia had been nice and sweet, so Kellan couldn't exactly tell her that the thought of marrying her kept waking him up with cold sweats—once he'd thrown up. He'd been saying that he wanted to make their wedding night special to explain away the fact that he hadn't been able to get his dick hard enough to fuck her for the last month. So when she started picking out dresses, he'd brought some of his douchiest friends down to Miami, hit the skankiest clubs, downed Jäger mixed with Blast until he couldn't think, and let nature take its course. This way Delia could tell herself she was lucky she found out now, be mad instead of crying. And hey, at least his dad should have been happy that he'd been out proving the fine qualities of Blast brand energy drinks, ensuring the family fortune.

Kellan would be a little more freaked about his dick's performance than about why he didn't want to marry a sweet girl who loved him, except he hadn't had any trouble getting off between the lips of that waitress—or between those huge tits.

"So dad starts going on about the cost of the ring—"

Nate's eyebrows shot up in disbelief.

"Well, I couldn't ask for it back. And it was fifty grand. But then with her dad being a senator and the national bottle deposit shit happening—"

"Yeah, that's a crisis, all right. Actually expecting companies to stop fighting recycling so we don't end up on Planet Garbage."

Talking about his dad's company wasn't the best way to get Nate on his side.

"So this morning he made me come over to the office in Dundalk to see him."

"Made you?"

Nate couldn't get it. Would never get Kellan's dad. Nobody said no to Geoffrey Brooks. Not till today. And still Kellan hadn't managed to spit it in the old man's face.

"Told me, whatever. When I got there, he started in on me about wasting my life and not accepting responsibility, and how I never had to work for anything in my life."

"Shit, now you've made me agree with your father. Just when I thought I couldn't hate you more."

"Yeah, well, I don't even think you would say you wished I'd never been born because I'll never live up to Keegan."

Nate bit his lip and looked away. "No, I wouldn't have said that."

"It's not like I didn't know he was always thinking it. He finally said it." Kellan managed a shrug while the words still

20

churned through him, stirring a rage he'd never known he could feel. Worse than what his father had said was the idea he'd put there, that Kellan had done something to dishonor Keegan.

Kellan remembered a lot about his brother Keegan. How tall he'd been. The way he could throw Kellan in the air, like he did when he got home from school every day. The Keegan in his head didn't look anything like the somber picture of him in his uniform next to the boxed American flag that was always on the display wherever his mom was living.

Nate came along after the Brooks family moved away from the house with "too many memories." Nate had only ever met Keegan next to the stone in the cemetery.

Catching Kellan's eye, Nate asked, "Then what? Your dad threw you out? He's done that before."

"Not like this. None of my credit cards work. He told me the house is off limits, that he'd changed the codes and would have me arrested for trespassing. He said the same thing about any of my cars. They're all in his name because—"

"You still don't have a license?"

"It got suspended again. But I wasn't drunk this time, man. This was for speeding."

Nate's lips flattened in a thin line. If he had been sorry for what Dad had said about wishing Kellan had never been born, it was all over now. Nate probably never got a parking ticket. Kellan stroked Quan Yin under her chin and poked at the puddle under his beer.

"Again, why are you here?"

"The old man said he'd give me one last chance before he washed his hands of me. If I could show some responsibility— like prove that I could do something without fucking it up—"

21

"Like what?"

"He said a lot of shit. Stuff like 'get a steady job' and 'stop whoring around.'" Then he said the something that had Kellan determined to throw it all back in his face. "Oh, and he says, 'Maybe some woman will take pity on you and try to make you a man. God knows I couldn't.' Fuck him." Quan Yin jerked her head away at the growl in Kellan's voice and then licked his wrist as if to tell him to calm down.

"So what the hell does that have to do with me?"

"Geoffrey thinks he wins." Kellan rubbed around the cat's ears as he dug in his back pocket for the piece of paper his father's secretary had handed him this morning. "That I'm going to follow his little action plan like one of his cubicle slaves. He's in for a shock. What would make him shit his drawers more than anything?" He looked steadily at Nate. "What kind of organizations can always count on Brooks Blast Energy Drinks for a donation?"

Nate's eyes widened. He'd never been slow to figure stuff out. "That's why you wanted a boyfriend?"

"Uh-huh. I'm going to find someone to make a man out of me. A gay man. Geoffrey Brooks, CEO of the most homophobic corporation in America, will now have an out and proud gay son."

Chapter Three

For a second, the possibility shone as bright as Christmas morning in the most consumption-driven advertisement Nate had ever seen. He could screw Kellan Brooks and his gay-hating, environment-destroying father at the same time. One for fun, one for revenge. Except they'd both be for revenge. Nate could always come up with a reason for fucking, but revenge wasn't a particularly good one. And there was that gigantic obstacle staring him in the face.

Kellan wasn't gay.

"Great plan. Let me know how it works. I've got about a hundred bucks in cash. Take it, wave it around at The Arena and someone will suck your cock and video it. Forget the cash, just take off your shirt and I'm sure someone will do you for free. Have fun."

"That's not the plan."

"Trust me. It'll work. The papers will run with it."

Kellan shook his head and kept petting Nate's quisling cat.

"Really, man. This is my job. Hell, I'll even print an article on your coming out."

"He'll only think I'm drunk."

"So what's your plan?" The question was uncomfortably familiar. How many times had Kellan proposed a plan when they were kids? How many times had Nate pointed out all the flaws in it? How many times had they gone and done it anyway?

"You."

"No."

"It's perfect." Kellan unfolded the paper he'd tossed on the counter, smoothing it over the condensation ring from his beer.

Nate picked it up and shook it dry while wiping down the counter around Quan Yin, whose look of exasperated resignation was almost a match for Kellan's.

Kellan snatched the paper back and put it on the now-dry countertop. "See? Under personal?"

As an editor, Nate had no trouble reading upside down, sideways or on the back of a receipt, but Kellan read the action plan aloud.

"All physical conduct with the opposite sex is to be conducted in private. No public drunkenness. Maintain a fixed address and contribute to household expenses if dwelling is shared. Proof of expenses paid required—cancelled checks or bank statements."

Nate pointed from his side of the counter. "You left off the part about stay out of the papers."

"Yeah, well, it won't be with a member of the opposite sex, and I won't be drunk."

"Somehow I don't think that's going to make Geoffrey happy."

"Good," Kellan said.

"Exactly what fixed address are we talking about?" Nate was pretty sure he knew what fixed address Kellan was thinking about.

"With you."

Nate arched his brows.

Kellan looked over his shoulder. "I'll sleep on the couch."

"You'll have to share."

Kellan beamed at the cat. "With this beautiful lady? No problem."

"With me."

Kellan glanced from the couch to Nate.

"The couch is my bed. It folds out. It's a studio apartment."

"Oh. I could— We could— It wouldn't be that long."

On the queen-sized mattress, Yin barely left enough room for Nate. He couldn't see the three of them crammed there.

"I'll sleep on the floor," Kellan said. "Or get an air mattress."

"You said you were broke."

"I could get a job."

"Doing what?"

"I don't know. Something."

"Kellan, I'm sorry all this shit happened to you—"

"No, you're not. You think I deserved it."

"Yeah, I do. But even if I didn't, you couldn't stay here. If you really want to do this, there are lots of other guys in Baltimore—some that would probably do it for kicks."

"None of them are you."

For the second time today Nate was breathing beer. He held up his hand to stop another assault on his back. Kellan didn't mean it like that. He probably had known Nate was headed there when they were thirteen, that Nate had a crush on him, and that more than anything had sent Kellan screaming into above-average adolescent male homophobia, but that was half a lifetime ago. No way could Kellan have meant that the way it sounded.

"Me being with you would make Geoffrey shit pinecones,"

25

Kellan explained when Nate stopped coughing.

Nate's ass clenched involuntarily at the image, but he had to admit Kellan was right.

"Especially after everything you've put in your column about him."

"You've read it?" "Shades of Gray", Nate's weekly column, hadn't put him in a position to get picked up by more than The Huffington Post, and his Queertiquette advice section definitely wasn't making Dan Savage nervous about his empire. The idea that Kellan Brooks had actually read Nate's column made him feel...something his overachieving vocabulary couldn't find a word for.

"Sometimes." Kellan shrugged. "You're funny. A lot funnier than I'd have thought, knowing you."

"Thanks." Whatever that unnamed feeling had been, it was gone now.

"So, will you help me put the screws to my father?"

"There's a lot more to being gay than simply saying you are and then moving in with a guy."

"You always say being gay isn't just about sex."

So Kellan *had* been reading Nate's stuff.

"It isn't only about that. But yeah, having sex with guys is a big part of it too."

Kellan stopped petting Yin, and she wandered off to the edge of the counter where she turned her back on both of them and began grooming herself. After they ignored the giant elephant dick in the room by watching the cat ignore them, Kellan finally pasted on a big smile.

"I'd do it."

"What?"

"If that's what it takes, if that will convince you—my dad,

the papers, whatever—I'll do it."

"Do what?"

"Have gay sex."

Kellan was bluffing. They might have been too young for poker when they were friends, but Nate knew Kellan was bluffing. He'd seen too many pictures of Kellan with D-list, D-cup actresses over the years to doubt the guy being anything but a one on the Kinsey scale.

Nate didn't do straight boys. But he'd called lots of bluffs.

"Really. You're going to have gay sex just to get back at your dad."

"Gay, straight. I thought there wasn't supposed to be a difference."

Nate came around the end of the counter and stood in front of Kellan. "Oh, there's a difference." Nate ran his hand down the fly of his jeans. "A big one if you're lucky."

Kellan got those two bright red spots high on his cheeks, but he didn't back down. "Well, obviously the other guy has a dick too, but a hole's a hole, right?" He swallowed, making Nate want to set his teeth in the thick bob of Kellan's throat.

"Not if the other guy's a top. You think fucking will feel the same when you're the one with a dick inside you? Exactly who do you plan to be having this gay sex with?"

Kellan didn't lose his smile, but there was a hardness to his face now. The way he'd been when he got back that summer and turned into a stranger. "I'll have it with you. C'mon, bro. You've had a hard-on for me since you figured out how to work your dick. This must be like waking up in a candy store." Kellan used his bigger body to back Nate against the counter until their hips were almost touching. "Suck anything you want."

Nice raise, but Nate still had the winning hand. He grabbed

27

Kellan's hips and ground them together. "Sucking is nice. Be my guest."

"Oh, I knew you had it bad for me." Kellan breathed the words into Nate's ear. "Did you jerk off thinking about me?"

Nate shoved his hand between them. "And I suppose this is a roll of quarters in your pocket." He found the thick length of Kellan's cock and stroked it.

Kellan jerked away. "Friction's friction."

"That's what I thought." Nate put his elbows on the counter behind him. "If you're going to play gay chicken, you'd probably be better off playing it with someone who isn't actually gay."

"I'm not chicken."

"Yeah? Gonna prove it?" Nate undid the top three buttons on his fly. The pulse in his cock probably had more to do with anger than arousal, but he was going to win this round. Nate hated Geoffrey Brooks on general principal, but Kellan's betrayal had been personal. "How desperate are you for a place to stay?"

"What are you saying?"

"I told you what I wanted in the bar."

Kellan wiped his hands on his thighs and then shrugged. "Okay."

"Just like that?"

"Like it's some big deal. I'd do my own if I could reach it." Despite his words, Kellan simply stood there.

Nate arched his brows. "That's all you got or were you waiting for kneepads?"

"Fuck you." Kellan dropped to his knees, eyeing Nate's crotch like he was waiting for it to attack.

Kellan would back down now, Nate was sure of it, but he threw in another taunt. "Afraid of trouser snakes?"

"Shut up, asshole." Kellan popped the last two buttons of Nate's fly.

"Why did it have to be snakes?" Nate teased.

They'd watched *Raiders* together a million times, skipping over the boring romance bits, replaying the explosions on slow speed. The line used to always make them laugh, but with Kellan's breath hitting the thin layer of cotton over Nate's dick, he wasn't laughing. Kellan's smile flashed for a second and was gone.

Seven years of being closer than Nate imagined even brothers could be told him to back off, to reassure Kellan he could stay as long as he needed provided he forgot this stupid plan. But those years melted into nothing stacked against the memory of that one year of eviscerating betrayal, of hearing Kellan's laugh behind the taunts of *faggot* and *queer* as Nate got tripped or shoved into lockers by someone who always disappeared when he turned around.

Nate took the last step and shoved his jeans and boxer briefs out of the way. His dick wasn't totally convinced it was about to get some action, so he gave it a couple of strokes, concentrating on the shape of the lips, the angle of the waiting jaw. A man's face. His cock. It would work. "Put up or shut up, Brooks."

Kellan licked his lips, nothing but nerves in the flicker of his tongue, but Nate imagined that first wet touch on his skin. That did the trick, a sweet flood of blood swelling him until the head stretched toward Kellan's mouth.

Nate put his elbows back on the counter and waited. Everything else was up to Kellan.

Chapter Four

Kellan swallowed and licked his lips again. He could do this. It wasn't that big a deal. Like Nate said, it was only a game of gay chicken, and no matter what, Kellan was going to win. He reached out and wrapped his hand around the shaft, ignoring how weird it felt to be holding a dick not his own. Wrong angle, wrong hold, but he still expected to feel the grasp on him because in some ways it was the same, satiny skin and heat and the pulse underneath. He jacked the shaft once, and then went for it. Nothing half-assed either. He did that thing he liked, where chicks kept their lips closed and slid the tip back and forth, let it glide across his cheek and then back to his lips.

Nate shifted, a gasp slipping from his throat. Oh yeah, Kellan was going to win.

He'd tasted his own come—off a girl's lips and once off his hand as a curious kid. Nate tasted—smelled—different than Kellan did too.

"Not bad." Nate wasn't gasping anymore. "I hate to break it to you if that's all the head you've been getting, but if you're going to blow me, you have to open your mouth."

Kellan looked up, and the way Nate was staring down dropped a heavy weight onto the squirming sensation in Kellan's gut. If Nate gave that look to all the guys about to suck his dick, no wonder he was so desperate to get done. His eyes were narrowed like he was pissed, his lips thin, flat, shut tight. Opening his mouth, Kellan tucked his lips over his teeth and went down hard and fast.

He choked and backed off, eyes watering from the bitter taste and the quick gag in his throat. Crossing his eyes, he tried to see how much dick he'd managed to get wet since he hadn't come close to hitting his fingers where they wrapped around the shaft. Shit. It was practically nothing. How the fuck did girls manage it? Kellan's dick was longer, though he thought Nate's was thicker. Maybe that was it. Too thick. He licked around the head, and the taste was mostly salt now.

He licked again, and then wrapped his lips right around what Keegan had told his curious baby brother was the helmet of his little soldier. Nate groaned so deep Kellan felt it echo in his belly. Then Nate's hands smacked into the sides of Kellan's head, shoving him off and away.

Kellan had barely regained his balance before the front door slammed behind Nate. The sound echoed around the apartment as Kellan sat back on his heels. "I guess that means I win," he told the empty room.

Nate had never been great at repressing anything. He'd taken his first psychology course to earn early college credit during his junior year of high school. When he'd heard about hiding problems under a metaphoric rug in his brain, he was the only one in class who couldn't relate. Nate was always too busy sweeping out the dust to let anything hide.

But after what he'd just done to another human being, he gave repression, rationalization and outright denial his best shot. He sprinted down the stairs, slamming against the wall and the handrail as he tried to do up his pants, started his scooter and took off down the sidewalk going the wrong way, fighting the accusations screaming in his head with every step. But there was no denying it. He was a rapist. Nate Gray, columnist, assistant editor of *Charming Rag*, *Baltimore's Premier Alternative Weekly*, was a fucking rapist.

He'd taken classes in every ism known to sociology and knew there was no excuse for such a blatant abuse of an unbalanced power dynamic. He pictured one of the separatist wimmin from his Feminist Analysis of Twentieth Century Literature course sharpening a blade for his imminent castration. If it wasn't Nate's equipment she planned to render inoperative, he'd have supplied her with the whetstone.

Desperate to distance himself from his own behavior, he tried framing it as a letter to his advice column.

Hey Gray,

My dad threw me out of the house, so I went to see an old friend. He said I could stay with him if I blew him. What do you think I should do?

Homeless

Hey Homeless,

There's a word, a legal word, for coercing someone into sex. That word is rape. Run. If he contacts you, call a cop.

Except he had been the one to run.

A pathetic whining excuse in his head tried to purify some of the guilt. Nate hadn't forced Kellan, hadn't so much as touched him. No one had pushed Kellan to his knees. He wouldn't have gone that far if he hadn't wanted to. For all Nate knew, the whole thing was some bizarre initiation game in some weird heterosexual conspiracy in straight men's endless quest to humiliate gay men. Kellan had definitely earned his way into that club.

Maybe if Nate was out of the apartment long enough, Kellan would disappear back into his own life. There had to be someone to take him in. Someone who wouldn't demand a blowjob as a rent payment. Someone who wasn't a despicable rapist.

And if he was still there, well, Nate's conscience would have to scrub itself clean by letting Kellan stay there as long he needed. And Nate's libido was going to have to find a way to live with that.

Chapter Five

Kellan licked his lips, still tasting Nate's come, the skin of his dick. Nate probably figured Kellan would be dashing to the sink to scrub the evidence from his mouth, and Kellan would have thought he would too, but it wasn't like they'd gotten far. If either of them was honest, it wasn't the first time one of them had had his dick out when they were together. They'd dressed together after sleepovers, gone skinny-dipping, and when Kellan had finally managed to shoot his first load right after he turned twelve, he'd gone running to tell Nate about it, fucking showed him how until Nate could do it too.

Not that what had happened back then—or that other time—was anything like today, but Kellan didn't feel any need to wash away gay cooties. All he felt at the moment was hungry, vaguely turned on in the kind of way he would be at the thought of getting some later, but mostly hungry. The beer he'd sipped while they talked sloshed around his empty stomach.

He rolled to his feet, stomped over, yanked open the fridge door and glared at a whole lot of empty space. He sure as hell hoped Nate would come home from his freakout with some food.

As a kid, Nate had been eerily neat, so it wasn't too much of a shock to find the fridge clean, but Kellan had expected that there would be some sign of edible food in there. Nate wasn't some stick-thin model living on sips of lemon-flavored water.

Instead Kellan found a jar of brown rice—uncooked—another jar of uncooked oatmeal and one with a tan paste, the beer—thank God—and some nectarines and grapes. Back then, Nate had loved pizza and Chinese buffets and burgers. When did Nate become a health freak?

The answer came easy.

Some time in the fifteen years since you stopped being his friend.

Kellan would find a way to make it up to him—or at least pay him back for this. Though he hoped it wouldn't involve any more seriously awkward blowjobs.

A check of the cabinets showed more tasteless things with labels like organic and healthy and whole grain taking up lots of space on the front. There was some tea, but Kellan didn't need to be hyper and hungry. He pushed the doors closed again. The cabinet next to the sink squeaked when he opened it, and Yin trotted over with a hopeful meow. He shrugged at her and then opened one of the cans of cat food onto a dish. The smell reassured him that he wasn't hungry enough to fight her for her ocean whitefish and salmon entree.

He didn't actually think there'd be any better food behind the door in the hall, but he looked anyway. Coats, a couple of suits and a worn guitar case. He didn't remember Nate going in for band or anything. Probably played—whatever kind of music went with granola and gay.

If he forced himself to answer, Kellan would say he was snooping around to distract himself from his empty stomach, but he knew damned well he was looking for some idea of who Nate was now. What he'd kept from back then, what he'd let go of.

So far he had liking animals, being neat and staying decent enough to not throw Kellan's ass onto the street. That was the

Nate he remembered. Nate's computer bag was next to the desk, but since a park bench would make a worse bed than this hardwood floor, Kellan didn't go that far in his search. Instead he opened the drawers. More signs of OCD neatness, paper, pencils and pens and paper clips in trays, but in the bottom right drawer, he hit a jackpot. A folder overfull of newsprint and the edge of a photo sticking out. Kellan tugged it until he could see more of it. Nate and his parents in some restaurant, Nate in a suit with his mom and dad. Based on Nate's age, Kellan was guessing college graduation, but his mom and dad looked thirty years older than Kellan remembered them.

Kellan slid the picture back inside the folder and tipped his head upside down so he could see to the back of the drawer without disturbing anything.

"Score," Kellan whispered to the empty apartment.

He got his fingers on the box he'd spied back there, and even before he pulled it out to where he could see it, Kellan knew what he'd find. Berger cookies. Baltimore's best. Vanilla cookies covered with an inch of chocolate frosting. Kellan grabbed two and stuffed them in his mouth before tucking them back out of sight. The rich buttercream reassured more than his empty stomach. Nate hadn't changed that much. He'd always been a sweets hoarder, like eating candy or cookies in public was some kind of sin.

Somewhere downstairs a door slammed. Kellan jumped like he'd been stealing cash instead of a few cookies. When the thunk of solid feet hit the wooden stairs, he ran for the bathroom and shower like his ass was on fire. It wasn't so much that he needed to hide evidence of sneaking into Nate's stash, but Kellan needed a few minutes to get ready for whatever was going to happen when Nate came in.

As Kellan backed into the spray, his hand reached for the

first bottle of gel it could find. For an ancient-looking place, the apartment had good water pressure. Hot needles beat relaxation into his shoulders. Now that he was wet and naked, his neck and back weren't the only things that would be better off with a release of tension. Looking down at his dick reminded Kellan of the grinding they'd done. It had been good enough to get the usual reaction from close contact with another human body. But when he'd knelt in front of Nate, Kellan's junk couldn't seem to make a collective decision about whether it was time to play or duck and cover. Then Nate had made that sound when Kellan licked him...

Maybe if he took advantage of the time to give his little soldier some R&R, neither of them would be thinking about how far he'd deviated from a straight line when he was on his knees. Or how flexible his dick was about what would make it jump up and salute. Because Kellan couldn't remember it ever getting that interested in the sound of a man's gasp tearing out of a stretched-taut neck. That his dick didn't care that the sex-moan sound was the result of Kellan having his lips on another man's cock was something he wasn't sure would wash away just by draining his balls. Especially not when the climb up to shooting kept filling his head with the hoarse sound Nate had made and the way his eyes had drifted closed, and how right it had felt to shove Nate up against the counter.

When Nate let himself back into the apartment, the room was empty, but the sound of the shower had him muttering, "Fuck" and trying to paste on a calm he didn't feel before he put the bags on the counter.

Dragging himself toward the bathroom door, he called, "I'm back."

No answer. Fuckety fuck. What if Kellan really did feel all

victimized and was hiding in the shower to avoid more assault?

Nate couldn't picture Kellan cowering from anyone. He was too fucking arrogant for that. Besides, it wasn't as if Kellan couldn't defend himself from Nate. Rape didn't have to be about physical power, his feminist studies reminded him.

"I got some stuff," Nate tried in a louder voice.

"Food?" Kellan's voice seemed normal.

"Yeah."

"Thank God." The water shut off, and Nate leapt back from the door like it was radioactive. He retreated to the kitchen and got out some chopsticks for the noodle bowls he'd picked up at Thai Supreme.

Wearing nothing but a towel that clung precariously to his hips, Kellan sauntered over to the counter. He sure wasn't acting like he had anything to fear.

Nate sucked in his breath, thankful he hadn't already started eating. He wasn't sure his respiratory system could handle any more inhalation of fluid along with his air.

Maybe Kellan prancing around like that was his way of dishing out payback. Or maybe it was a hell of a karmic kick to the nuts. Either way, Nate was feeling good and punished, the scourge of unrequited lust doing worse to him than his conscience ever could. Oh yeah, thirteen-year-old Nate had had a crush on his best friend, but the memory was purely emotional.

This was lust.

Nate had never thought he had a type. He'd dated all kinds of guys, found lots of them hot enough to take to bed. But he sure as hell had a type now.

Kellan Brooks.

Kellan Brooks standing in Nate's kitchen with lickable

drops rolling down his sculpted abs. A drop caught in a line of hair that started in the middle of his rib cage to darken a few inches before it disappeared under the edge of the towel.

He'd stared for no more than a split second before Nate turned his focus to the fascinating clumps of soba noodles wrapping around the tofu in his bowl, but the image burned into his brain with indelible clarity. Whatever kind of fun Kellan was wasting his life having, it wasn't doing much harm to his body. With clothes on, Kellan was tall, seeming thin and rangy, but there was no absence of muscle on his frame. He would have made a Renaissance sculptor crawl over broken stained glass for a chance to use him as a permanent model.

Kellan looked in the container he'd uncovered and then back at Nate. "What's that?"

"A noodle bowl. It's like a Thai stew or soup."

"Yeah? Chicken?" Kellan's nose wrinkled in suspicion.

"It's tofu."

Kellan looked in both of the other bags then sighed. "Why?"

"I'm a vegetarian."

"Since when?"

"Since the amount of water wasted to raise a beef cow is equivalent to the yearly use of a family of four. Since many animals are still alive when they are processed for their—"

Kellan held up a hand. "Fine. Tofu. Whatever. I'm so hungry I don't care what I put in my mouth."

That doomed Nate's diaphragm to another round of eye-watering coughs and gasps. The matching pair of familiar dark red spots burst high on Kellan's cheeks, but by the time Nate had his breath back, Kellan was offering a twisted smile.

"Just so you know, the idea of tofu is worse. Isn't it like scum off of beans? You know I hate beans."

"You hate string beans. This is different."

Kellan picked up the chopsticks. "Still beans, man."

Nate waited to see if Kellan would have to ask for a spoon and fork, but he scooped up noodles and vegetables and stuffed them into his mouth without difficulty. Nate tried to pretend he wasn't disappointed that Kellan didn't need standard utensils.

Next up was trying to pretend he wasn't looking at the expanse of chest across the counter, at the dark pebbled skin around brick-red nipples that had Nate biting his tongue to stem his need to find out what they tasted like.

He looked back at his noodle bowl, but the bean sprouts reminded him of sperm and that was no help. Silently begging Yin to leap up and create a distraction didn't work.

He felt fifteen again, popping wood because the breeze rubbed him right. But this wasn't a breeze. This was Kellan. Grown-up, sexy, untouchable Kellan. And Nate deserved every unfulfilled tingle and pulse in his dick, every ache in his balls that wanted to paint that chest with streaks of his come. Deserved feeling like he was wearing some kind of cock-and-ball torture chastity harness because of how he'd treated Kellan.

Kellan dropped his chopsticks as his hand went to his hip to grab the towel.

Nate seized on that with relief and shoved one of the bags toward Kellan. "I grabbed some sweats for you while I was out. Hope they fit."

Kellan tipped his head. "Oh? Thought maybe part of me staying here would mean I had to walk around naked."

Nate would have been perfectly content to die on the spot, hard-on and all.

"Or maybe you wanted to reciprocate? Isn't that how you guys do it?"

The comment would have provoked a corrosive sneer about generalizations and heterosexual assumptions and obsessions with gay sex if Nate wasn't drowning in guilt.

Unclenching his teeth, he forced out, "If you really need a place to stay—"

"Your dick in my mouth wasn't enough to prove how desperate I am?"

"Okay, fine. You can stay here until you find someplace else to stay. The rest of that—" His back teeth slammed together so hard he thought they'd shatter. It was too dangerous to play games. The want burning in Nate was enough to make him forget anything he'd ever learned about power and abuse. There'd be no more touching—not even if they were only screwing around. He'd help Kellan until he had a job and a place of his own, and that would be it. Kellan would be gone, and once Nate wasn't burning alive with frustrated lust, he'd be able to concentrate on constructing a coherent sentence again.

"That stuff." Nate gestured downward. "It was a game. You won. That's it. All right?"

"What about the rest of it?"

"What about it?"

"My plan to put old Geoffrey in his place."

"Look, being gay is not like dying your hair blue to freak out your parents. It's not something you can play with like that."

"So you get to call that stuff..." Kellan mimicked Nate's gesture, "...a game, but I can't play."

Nate ignored him. "You can't be gay because it's convenient. It's not what sexuality is about."

"Is it?"

"What?"

"Convenient. Is being gay convenient?"

At the moment, being attracted to men—with this one standing in front of him—was as far from convenient as Nate ever hoped to get. So far from convenient that he couldn't come out from behind the counter, couldn't move without waddling with that spike in his jeans.

He scooped up more noodles. "No. Gay is what I am. It's not something you decide to wear for a while and then throw it out when you're done."

"What if I make it worth your while?" Kellan arched his brows.

"I told you that was a game. I don't want to have sex with you, Kellan."

Nate couldn't decide which called him a liar loudest, his balls, his dick or the look in Kellan's eyes, so he concentrated on finishing his supper.

"That's not what I'm offering. You say you won't do this just to get back at my dad. Even after what he did to yours. What if it wasn't only about my dad? What if I could tell you something that would prove some of that stuff in your column about the South District deal being a fake? Proof to get the whole mess shut down?"

Geoffrey Brooks had promised that his company's expansion into vitamin water would use the waste in the district for power and reopen the abandoned bottling plant to create ten thousand jobs—in exchange for millions in tax concessions from the city. The deal was set to go down in September. "Real proof?"

"Papers, emails, blueprints, budget statements. He's already bought a plant in China for the bottling."

"Are you bullshitting me?"

"No, but you're not getting the proof till I get what I want. Here's what's on the table. You get to make Geoffrey Brooks's head explode, possibly causing several bigoted politicians and media moguls to cut off contact with him—or not take his donations—and in the end, you get the big prize, Geoffrey's big-deal scam blows up in his face and you save the city. Like Superman."

"Batman's cooler," Nate said. "And what's my end of the bargain?"

Kellan's cheeks got those two dark patches of color. Did he really think Nate would bring up sex again? "Um."

"In exchange for what?" Nate clarified.

"You pretend to be my boyfriend. Wait—you help me pretend that we're madly in love."

It wasn't as if Nate didn't owe Geoffrey Brooks a gigantic knee to the balls. And it wasn't only personal. In the end, those tax concessions would cost more jobs than they were clearly going to get. Would it be so bad to let Kellan fake coming out?

"How long are we talking?" Nate said.

"I don't think it should be longer than a month or two— hell, maybe Geoffrey will be kissing my ass in a week."

"What if he doesn't give a shit? Then what are you going to do?"

"Well, that'll be my problem again, won't it?"

There were no more noodles to fish out of the bowl. "Two months."

"Deal."

Kellan had left most of the tofu swimming in the broth, and most of the vegetables and the noodles. He scooped out some and eyed them suspiciously before sliding them into his mouth. "How long have you been doing this vegetarian shit?"

"Since I went to college."

"It's a total crime. Man, your mom made the best sausage and beef lasagna in the world."

Back when they could afford it. After Geoffrey Brooks's betrayal, Nate's dad had lost his job. Too many times his mom or dad had sat in front of an empty plate at the dinner table, saying, "Go ahead, son, I'll get something later." Nate hadn't realized until he was seventeen that they were taking food off their own plates to feed him.

That lasagna had been amazing, and now his parents could afford it again. "Yeah."

"How is your mom?"

"She's fine. They live out in Catonsville now." Nate couldn't resist the chance to remind Kellan why it had been so long since he'd had Mom's lasagna. "She used to ask me why you never came to the house anymore. She wanted me to tell you you were always welcome."

Kellan shifted his weight from foot to foot and dropped his chopsticks into the bowl. "I bet she didn't wonder long."

"If Geoffrey could have seen your negotiation skills just now, convincing me to help you, he'd probably set you up as a vice-president tomorrow."

"Would that be with or without the blowjob part of the negotiation?"

It killed Nate to admit it, but as long as Kellan had that stupid mistake to hold over him, he was always going to win. Nate folded his arms and nodded at Kellan's bowl. "You done with that?"

"Yeah. All done with seaweed and bean scum."

"Well, maybe tomorrow you can find a job and buy your own food. But don't bring any meat into the house."

The downstairs door buzzed, the intercom giving Eli's voice a rasp he'd never manage on his own. "Nate? It's me."

Kellan snatched the bag holding the sweatpants off the counter. "Guess if company's here I'd better go wrap up the one kind of meat you like." The bathroom door slammed behind him.

Chapter Six

Kellan kept the bathroom door open a crack as he pulled the baggy sweats up his legs so he could get a handle on who Nate's company was. When Kellan came up with his plan, he'd never stopped to wonder if Nate already had a boyfriend. Nate wouldn't have agreed if he did, right?

The apartment door opened and a guy with a singsong voice and a British accent said, "What happened to you, Nate? Thought we were out on the pull tonight, you and me. Said we'd meet at J.J.'s."

"Christ, Eli, in three sentences you've gone from East London to Birmingham to Oxford. If you're going to fake an accent to get laid, you might want to stick to one county. You're not the only person who gets BBC America with basic cable."

Kellan did. Back in his bedroom suite, on the fifty-six inch flat screen. He even watched the channel enough to know what *on the pull* meant. Too bad Nate was about to get cock-blocked. This might be fun after the way Nate had to go and bring up Geoffrey again.

"Yeah, like you're the fucking expert, Mr. One Semester at Oxford." Eli didn't like Nate's know-it-all shit any more than Kellan did.

"Cambridge."

"What-the-fuck-ever." Eli would make his point better if he

didn't whine.

"I'd explain it, but we'd be here all night." No wonder Nate lived alone. With a head that big there wasn't room for anyone else. "C'mon."

"Whose shoes are those? Did you already get lucky?" Eli couldn't have given Kellan a better opening if he'd handed the guy a script. "Jesus, those shoes are huge. Is he hung? Did you let him—?"

Kellan tugged the sweats until they barely clung to his hips and put on the swagger he'd picked up when he'd been dating that girl who was on one of the CW soaps. Popping open the bathroom door, he charged up behind Nate and slung an arm around his neck. "Hey, baby, who's this?"

Eli turned out to be a few inches shorter and a whole lot skinnier than Nate, with black hair hanging in gray eyes that turned silver-bright with the black eyeliner around them. His skin looked smooth like a girl's, lower lip pouting enough to make Kellan's dick twitch in a way that had him thinking Eli knew how to work the whole gender-bending thing. Masculine jaw, but the cheeks and shiny lips, shit. Kellan didn't know if he should bump shoulders with the guy or compliment his shoes in order to get laid.

"Well, damn, he does fill out those...shoes." Eli's dark lashes dropped as he aimed an obvious look at Kellan's package. Eli wasn't doing the accent again, but his voice took on that singsong tone. "Eli Wright." He offered his hand.

Kellan kept his left arm hooked around Nate's shoulders as he returned the handshake. Eli's fingers were blunt, the grip strong, but the light caress on Kellan's wrist as Eli pulled his hand back made Kellan forget to offer his own name in greeting.

Eli added a wink. "You look really familiar. I know that sounds like a line, but I swear I've seen you somewhere."

"This is Kellan," Nate said as he detached Kellan's arm, but Kellan turned the motion into holding hands.

"His boyfriend," Kellan added with the first real grin he'd felt on his face all day. Damn that had been fun to say, especially the way Nate squeezed back like he'd break Kellan's fingers while Eli's pretty mouth turned into a perfect O as he gasped.

"That was fast," Eli said after a pause.

"We've—we've been having a long distance thing," Nate stammered. "But—"

"I hated being away from him all the time, so we decided to live together," Kellan cut in. Nate was going to need some practice lying. Kellan turned and kissed Nate's temple, getting a whiff of his hair. It smelled...good. Not like anything. Not like sweat or shampoo or cologne, just good.

"When?" Eli's question seemed kind of choked off, like there was more he wanted to ask but couldn't get it into words.

"This afternoon. Nate didn't even know I was coming to Baltimore. I'm a big surprise."

"Well, I guess that takes care of my next question." Eli was back to his pouty-lipped self.

"What was that?"

"I was going to ask if you wanted to fuck." Eli winked again, and his tongue made one hell of a promise before flicking back into his mouth.

Shock relaxed the grip Kellan had on Nate, and he freed his hand. Damn. If you could talk to girls like that, it would sure save a hell of a lot of time—not to mention cash and hangovers. Gay guys definitely had an advantage.

Nate saved Kellan from having to figure out how to answer that. "Eli."

"What?" Eli held up his hands. "The way you talked about tonight, I didn't figure you guys were exclusive or anything. But if Kellan just got here, I guess you guys will be busy."

"Hey, I don't want to wreck anyone's plans." Kellan shrugged and recaptured Nate's hand. "You guys go out like you were planning, and I'll crash. I'm kind of beat from the trip."

"Come with us," Eli offered.

Nate tried to free his hand again. "We should probably both stay in."

Kellan felt the tension making Nate's body rigid. What would it take to make him snap?

"You go, baby. You wore me out earlier." Kellan winked at Eli.

"Kellan." Eli raised his palm and gave his forehead an audible smack. "Fuck me, you're Kellan Brooks. Like Brooks Blast Energy Drinks. But how is that long distance? I thought you lived around here."

Kellan leaned back against the counter. "Well, you know my dad. Nate's been great about keeping a lid on things, but finally I said fuck it and had to be real, you know?"

Eli's eyes fluttered wide. "That is so amazing. What did your dad do?"

"Threw me out on my ass with nothing more than the clothes on my back."

"Wow." Eli looked from Kellan to Nate and blinked again. "You guys need a theme song or something. So that's why you've been watching all those websites and stuff. Weren't you engaged, like to a woman?"

"A beard." Nate suddenly came to life. "Okay, let's get moving. You rest up, honey." Nate's lips twisted in a smile that was almost three-quarters grimace. "I'll be back to wear you out again later."

Eli looked from Nate to Kellan like he was starting to think he'd missed the joke. Kellan hooked a finger through Nate's belt loop as he was about to disappear through the door. "What, no kiss goodbye?"

Nate glared a warning, but Kellan hauled him into a kiss anyway. As Kellan put his hands on either side of Nate's face, the bristles prickled his palm, but the hair in the full goatee was soft when Kellan put his lips on Nate's mouth. Nate softened for a second, maybe just for show, but Kellan couldn't resist the dare. He parted his lips and let his tongue slide along the seam of Nate's lips until with something like a growl, Nate opened his mouth.

Kellan slipped his tongue in and they were really kissing, soft at first, then Nate grabbed Kellan's ass and hitched him closer, mouth opening wider, hips grinding, and maybe this dare had gone a little too far. It didn't feel like kissing a girl, not even one who liked things a little rough. The tongue action might be almost the same, but there was no hiding the fact that Nate wasn't a girl, not with the strength in the grip that shifted to Kellan's hips, and definitely not with the tickle of that hair against his lips and cheek. Nate tipped up his jaw and moved one hand to the back of Kellan's head, the other a hard press on Kellan's waist. Nate's tongue slid past Kellan's to stroke and tease, and Kellan was having trouble remembering exactly why it had seemed like a good idea to push Nate's buttons.

Nate's hand slid down from Kellan's waist to cup his ass again, not the hard grip like before, but a teasing caress. Nate released Kellan's head. "Feel free to wait up for me, baby." Nate's voice was husky, teasing Kellan's ear like a brush of soft fingers. "You ready?"

For a second, Kellan thought Nate was talking to him, and though Kellan didn't know for sure what he was about to say he was ready for, he knew that those kind of kisses and a husky teasing voice were just how Nate managed to get himself laid.

Eli answered, "Uh, yeah. Okay. Are you sure you want to go?"

Now Kellan was the one who couldn't seem to figure out what to say.

"Yeah. I'm good." Nate winked at Kellan and stepped through the door.

Oh, he was, the sneaky bastard.

"I cannot believe you're fucking Kellan Brooks," Eli said for the hundredth time since they'd left the apartment.

Nate should know by now that even his fifth Smirnoff Ice wouldn't chase the tingle of that kiss off his lips. "Why is it so surprising? I fucked you once."

Eli hid his reaction under the fall of his bangs, and Nate buried a wince in the new bottle the bartender had put in front of him. He wasn't always such a mean drunk.

"Yeah, well everyone knows I'm easy," Eli shot back.

That had been a mistake. Kind of like feeding a stray. The paper had hired Eli as a photographer a couple months ago, and his flattery and sex-on-legs appeal had gotten Nate's dick up that sweet ass in about three days. He should have known better than to fuck a coworker and a young one at that—since Nate felt like the gap in their ages was closer to twenty years instead of the actual seven. Should have known that Eli's effervescent adoration would turn him into a barnacle Nate couldn't peel off. And it was his own fault for letting the flattery go to both his heads.

As Nate stared into the half-empty bottle of Smirnoff, he wondered if that was the way he'd made Kellan feel, smothered under the weight of too much attention. Was that what had driven him to be such a fucking dick that year?

Nate realized Eli was yelling something in his ear over the thumping mix from the DJ, something that didn't sound like his refrain of I can't believe you're fucking Kellan Brooks.

"What?" Nate yelled back, leaning closer.

"I said, 'What are you guys going to do now?' I mean, like about his dad? Is it a secret still?"

Some perverse part of Nate wanted to tell Eli that it was a secret, prolong the weird dynamic of a pretend version of the boyfriend Nate had dreamed of living with at thirteen, but he yelled back in Eli's ear, "No. Kellan's tired of being in the closet." God, they were really doing this. "He doesn't care what his dad does."

"That is so cool."

No, it was exploitative. What Kellan was doing was wrong. Nate started to say something, but Eli went on with that familiar infatuated gleam in his eyes.

"I can't believe he'd walk away from all that money. He's a hero. You should totally do something for the paper. I bet Jess could write up something really cool, not too corny."

That was exactly what Kellan wanted. Geoffrey would settle twenty million dollars on him the second the bigger papers picked the story up. Then Kellan could issue his *ha-ha, it was just a big joke* retraction. Everyone would believe it was another one of his stunts. And Eli and every other gay kid who'd ever had their parents tell them they were a disgusting mistake would take it like the gut punch it was. Nate was crazy to have agreed to this. "We'll think about it."

"But I get to do the shoot, right?"

"Yeah, I'll make sure."

"Thanks, Nate." Eli kissed him. "So you mind if I go dance?"

"I'll come with you." Maybe the beat pounding up through his bones would help him forget how fucked up everything was. Stop the plant or set back gay rights? Let Kellan keep playing gay chicken or stop testing the boundaries of consent?

Eli kept a good space between them, which was what Nate would expect for a guy showing off to garner some attention. Watching him dance, Nate remembered why he'd had Eli's pants around his ankles three days after he met him. He moved like he didn't have a spine, fluid, twisting, hips and ass inviting touch with every swivel. Nate turned away from repeat temptation and found himself staring at a shirtless chest, hard jaw and intent dark eyes. The other man rocked them together once, then stepped back, gaze dropping to Nate's crotch as he licked his lips and tipped his head in invitation.

Nate's lips might still be tingling from a kiss that had gotten out of hand, but his dick was rock hard at the promise in this stranger's eyes. He couldn't remember the last time he'd gotten off with someone.

He glanced back. Eli was dancing with another goth-like twink. He'd be fine. Better than fine if he'd stop chasing guys who were too old for him. Nate started to follow the other man through the crowd.

A hand yanked him back.

"Where are you going?" Eli yelled in his ear.

"To pee, all right?"

"No. You're going to get your dick sucked. I can't believe it. After everything he gave up for you?"

"Trust me. Kellan won't mind at all."

"You didn't see the way he looks at you."

"Jesus, Eli, mind your own fucking business." Nate wrenched himself away, but the tall, shirtless guy was gone. And he wasn't waiting by the men's room or anywhere else. Nate went back to the bar and downed another two bottles of Smirnoff Ice before Eli found him to deliver another lecture.

By the time Eli did find him, Nate was so smashed he had to transfer his grip from the edge of the bar to Eli's shoulder to stay on his feet.

"What the fuck is wrong with you, Nate? I mean, now I get why you've been such a bitch at work with this shit hanging over your head, but now you've got this amazing guy who gave up everything for you, and you're acting like a total fucking asshole."

"Oh yeah. He's amazing. I'm an asshole. Closest I'm getting to one for another fucking month anyway." Nate knew it was a stupid joke, but he laughed anyway.

"What?" Eli started to drag him out of The Arena.

"Nothing. Where'd your little doppelganger go?"

"I don't know. I've been looking for you."

"Go on. Get laid. At least one of us should."

"Did you guys get into a fight or something?"

"No. Just." Outside he took a breath of air misted with spring rain and straightened up. "Forget about me. Go back in."

"I'm not leaving you here like this for some bashers to find." Eli shoved Nate up against the bricks of the alley, holding him with one arm while digging through Nate's pockets. "Fuck me."

"You were really a good time, Eli, but I've got a lot on my...dick, right now." Nate laughed again, turning his face into the rain which was coming down harder.

"And you thought I was immature. Nate, I can't get you home like this. Do you have money enough for a cab on you?"

Nate shoved his hips forward. "S'all yours."

Eli reached in and grabbed Nate's wallet. "You are so going to owe me for this. You'd better not fuck things up with Kellan either." Eli dragged Nate out of the alley toward Eager Street.

The only consolation Nate could figure was that when he dropped into bed next to a sleeping Kellan Brooks—*please let him be sleeping*—Nate would be too drunk to suffer another round of blue balls.

Chapter Seven

A baby cried and jerked Kellan out of a sound sleep.

But there couldn't be a baby. He wasn't ready for a baby. And no matter how much Delia had talked about waiting, he knew she had the kids' names picked out and got this dreamy look when she saw a kid in a stroller on the street.

He lay there, heart pounding as he remembered where he was. Nate's place. He turned his head to look at the human lump next to him on the equally lumpy fold-out sofa bed.

Eli had poured Nate through the front door at about twelve thirty with a "It's not my fault" and a "He's all yours."

Kellan had spent enough nights on his knees in front of the porcelain god to know what the sudden grimace on Nate's face meant. Two hard shoves got him into the bathroom in time.

Kellan wet a towel and threw it at him, and Nate dragged himself onto the bed a few minutes later.

But there was still a baby crying. Not like in another apartment, but closer to Kellan's ear. He sat up and looked out of the window next to Nate. A streak of something lighter than the black caught his eye, and Kellan rolled out of bed and walked around to the window.

He'd left it open about three inches because the apartment was stuffy and Nate reeked. Somehow Quan Yin had managed to wriggle through the space and out onto the fire escape. The window had slid shut, she was crying, and it was raining again.

Kellan rolled onto the floor and held the sill up while he waved her in. "C'mon, sweetie."

She mewled again from her spot under the broad leaf of some plant sitting on one corner.

"C'mon, girl. You're only going to get wetter."

She huddled down and glared at him like he was responsible for the weather, the condition of her owner and the fact that she was out there getting wet in the first place. The last two might be his fault, but Kellan wasn't taking the blame for the weather. That was just Baltimore in April.

He shoved the lump on the bed. The only thing that made a sound were the springs that had been poking Kellan's back through the mattress.

"Nate. Your cat's stuck outside." Kellan pushed harder. "C'mon. She won't come in for me."

Nate's head shifted in time with another pitiful sound from his cat. "Sh'sfine."

"It's raining and she won't come in."

Nate made a completely indecipherable sound and started snoring.

Kellan sighed. The window had drifted shut again as he tried to wake up Nate.

He slapped it open and reached out for the cat who glanced at his hand disdainfully. The wind picked up in a way that told Kellan a downpour was on its way in T-minus ten seconds. The fire escape wasn't that long. He could reach her without having to climb out. He lay across the sill and stretched. She was just past the tips of his fingers, ears flat, crouched under the shelter of that leaf. Kellan wiggled farther.

Three things happened at once. His feet left the floor, the window frame crashed down on the backs of his knees, and a sudden slam of thunder split the air. Quan Yin jumped, the big pottery base of the plant tilted wildly and went over the edge of the fire escape, banging and crashing as it went, and Kellan's head and arms followed as he grabbed the cat before she went over too.

He kicked his legs, but the window was surprisingly heavy, and he didn't have much leverage with his arms full of angry wet cat. The rain was coming in waves from the bay, soaking them both in seconds. As he managed to tuck her close to his body, Yin stopped clawing at him. He kicked harder with his feet, but the sill didn't move. His abs strained to hold him above the fire escape.

None of the neighbors seemed perturbed about the crash of the planter into the backyard. Maybe they thought it was more thunder. He tried to angle his foot toward the bed and finally hit something hard and covered with skin.

He swung at it again.

Over the rush of water he heard a muttered, "Stop it," then at last, "Jesus Christ, Kellan, why're you kicking me?" Nate's voice got louder. "What the fuck are you doing?" Nate sounded a lot more alert as his hand landed on Kellan's calf.

The window came up off his legs, and Kellan slid back inside with Quan Yin. "I was saving your cat."

"She sits out there sometimes. She's fine."

"In a thunderstorm."

Nate blinked and rubbed his eyes. "Shit. You guys are really wet."

"This bulletin brought to you from the Department of Duh."

Nate shut the window behind them. The sound released the

cat from her temporary paralysis. She tore a strip of cotton from the T-shirt and a strip of skin from Kellan's stomach before springing away and disappearing somewhere in the apartment.

"Ow. You're welcome," Kellan called after her.

"That's my shirt," Nate blurted.

"Another brilliant observation. I borrowed it. Or did you want me sleeping naked?"

"Jesus, just stop it. Stop it." Nate collapsed on the bed, rubbing his forehead and eyes. "What time is it?"

"Almost five."

"My head is going to explode. And I have to be at work in two hours."

"Yeah, that'll happen if you pound back all those bitch drinks." Kellan leaned over and sniffed. "Blue Skyy or Smirnoff Ice?"

"Do you know how pathetic it is that you can figure that from smell?"

"I'm pathetic? Who's the one who drank so much of that crap that he's trying to hold his brains in his skull?"

"Shit." Nate clutched his head some more.

Kellan got up and found a towel, leaving the T-shirt behind in the basket in the bathroom. When he came back, Nate was still moaning and yanking at his hair like pulling it out would help his headache.

"So what made you want to get so wasted? Me or that pretty thing you went out with?"

"He's not a thing. He's a man. A hell of a better one than you."

Kellan rolled his eyes at that, but Nate kept going.

"When he was seventeen, his parents asked him if he was

gay. When he said he was, he came home from school to find a box of his stuff tossed in the driveway. They threw him out, and he had to beg for places to live for a year until he finished high school."

"Yeah, I think I can get that."

"No, you fucking don't." Nate came off the bed, winced and dropped back down. "They've never spoken to him again. That's his life, and you're playing a fucking game with it to get back at your dad because he hurt your feelings."

"God, Nathan, you are so fucking full of yourself I'm surprised you don't cause an earthquake when you shit."

"What?"

"Eli's parents are assholes, and that's my fault now? My dad fucked over yours, and that's my fault? Is there something else you want to blame on me?"

"Oh no. One thing's enough." Nate shoved himself off the bed again, wavered and then breathed that too-sweet vodka haze in Kellan's face. "You outed me to the whole school. You made my life a fucking hell until we moved away."

"You told me, you told your folks, I thought everyone knew."

"No. I only told you."

That day near the end of eighth grade, Kellan had come to school late because he had a dentist appointment and found Nate outside at lunch, cornered by three assholes yelling *Suck my dick, faggot* at him. Kellan had hit his growth spurt at eleven. At thirteen he still towered over the rest of the kids. One shove and they scattered. But Nate wouldn't look at him after. Wouldn't laugh at Kellan's jokes. Didn't say anything until they were up in Nate's room after school. "What if I am, Kell? I think maybe—"

"Check out this magazine I swiped from the dentist office." Kellan had shoved some picture of a bike flying off a dirt ramp in front of Nate's face to keep him from finishing that sentence. "Do you think we could make something like that? Back in the park on one of the trails?"

Nate had sighed and grabbed the magazine. "Yeah, maybe, but we'll need a lot of dirt and a way to pack it and something to make sure it doesn't erode the first time we use it."

Fifteen years later it was Kellan's turn to sigh. "Fine. You told me you were gay and I freaked out. But I didn't do any of that shit."

"Like write cocksucker on my locker or trip me or rip up my homework or keep me locked in a toilet stall full of piss and shit for all of third period?"

"You know I didn't." But he hadn't stopped it either. Didn't talk to Nate at all after coming home from camp that summer. Never met him back at the ramp they'd built.

Nate's breath came out in a grunt full of disbelief. "Great. I'm sure that makes everything fine in your world." He staggered toward the bathroom.

"Are we still doing this?" Kellan called after him.

"What?"

"The boyfriend thing."

"You mean am I going to let you use coming out, the single most important facet of gay consciousness, as a way to get back into your dad's pockets? Just on the off chance that you've got information that will keep the people in this city from being fucked over by some soulless corporation?"

What the fuck was gay consciousness? Being awake while you were fucking? "Well, yeah. But it's not a chance. I can get you the information you need."

"I'll think about it in the shower."

Chapter Eight

Nate put a dry towel on the floor for Yin and added laundry to the to-do list stretching toward infinity in his aching brain: detox, rehydrate, get more hairball gel for Yin, wash towels, help Kellan Brooks lie about his sexual orientation to get even with his father, change the litter box, call back one of the clubs that was dithering about keeping ad space in the paper, don't choke on your tea when Kellan walks out of the bathroom in nothing but a towel—

He reordered things. Buy Kellan some clothes moved to the top of the list.

Kellan wasn't wearing a towel, he had on the sweats, but it still left a lot of skin on display. Nate buried his expression in his mug of tea as Kellan opened and slammed cabinet doors in a nauseating rhythm.

"Where's the coffee? You get up at five the fuck o'clock in the morning and you don't have coffee? What do you have against coffee?"

Nate pictured a rich, creamy latte flowing over his lips as he sipped his bitter green tea. "Nothing, provided it's fair-trade and shade-grown. I don't happen to have any right now."

Kellan leaned over Nate's shoulder in a cloud of Nate's soap, clean man and mint toothpaste. Had Kellan—

"Did you use my toothbrush?" Nate asked.

"No. Rubbed with a finger. What's that?" Kellan leaned over farther and sniffed. "Looks like piss and smells worse."

"It's green tea."

Despite a clear path on the other side of the counter, Kellan squeezed by Nate, chest rubbing against Nate's arm.

"Tea's the last thing you need with a hangover, man. It's a diuretic. How do you not know that, Mr. Health Food?"

"I'm detox— Fuck it."

Kellan was right. Nate's pounding head and dry mouth led him to yank open the fridge, pop the filter top off the Brita and chug a quart right out of the pitcher.

"That's better. You got aspirin or Tylenol around here?"

Nate caught his breath and wiped his mouth on his hand. "End table next to the bed."

Kellan crossed over and opened the drawer. "What the— uh—okay."

Nate smiled at the flush on Kellan's cheeks. "I suppose you've never seen—"

"A dick in a drawer before? Not that I can remember. Do you—? Never mind." Kellan put the tiny bottle on the counter next to Nate's hand.

"Thanks. About coffee…"

"Yeah?" Kellan sounded hopeful and so much like his younger self Nate hated to disappoint him.

"I still don't have any, but I might have found you a job where you can have all you can drink."

"Starbucks?"

"No. Manna Café. I talked to the manager last night and—"

"Would that be before or after you got obliterated on sugar and vodka?"

"Before. She said you could stop by after the morning rush and she'd talk to you." Nate took a couple of Tylenol with another pint of water.

"Wow. Don't take this the wrong way, but you've got a lot in common with old Geoffrey."

"Gee, why would I take that the wrong way?" Nate almost slammed the pitcher on the counter but spared his head.

"You're both quick to manage my life."

"Kellan. According to you, you've got the clothes on your back. I said I'd give you a place to stay, but even if we go through with the whole fake-lovers thing, you're going to need some money. In case you haven't noticed, I'm not exactly rolling in it."

"If we go through with it?" Kellan hoisted himself up onto the counter, like he needed the extra height.

"I'm still not sure."

"Because of Eli?"

"Who said I wanted to date Eli?" Nate didn't want to date anyone. He only wished he could get laid more than once a month. Based on the letters people sent his advice column, relationships were almost a guarantee of not having sex. He used to have sex. Lots of sex. And then he got promoted right out of doing almost anything but work.

"Wow. Like *that's* not a sign of denial. But that's not what I meant. Before you acted like you thought he would get hurt by it, because of his folks."

Nate couldn't remember exactly what he'd been ranting about before he hit the shower, but that sounded about right.

"So we should ask him," Kellan said.

"He can't keep a secret. And there goes your plan."

"No, I mean hypothetically."

"Huh?"

"You went to college and you don't know what hypothetically means?"

"What, like you say, 'I have a friend who—'"

"Can you lie, I mean at all? Or are you always this painfully obvious?"

Nate didn't need to lie. That was the whole point of his life so far. Why he'd wanted to write for a paper in the first place, why he'd done all those special-interest stories and fluff pieces about bands and local talent so that he could get to write about stuff that mattered.

Eli must have some kind of psychic ability that let him have really accurate timing, because as Nate was sputtering in defense of honesty, Eli buzzed the apartment.

It wouldn't be the first time he'd dropped by with breakfast. But it would be the first time Nate was a hundred percent happy to see him.

At the mention of coffee over the intercom, Kellan sprang down the stairs to help Eli carry stuff up.

"I wanted to make sure you were all right. And you were the one who called a staff meeting for eight this morning." Eli opened a bakery bag and started handing out muffins.

"You wanted to know if we had a big fight," Kellan said around a mouthful of blueberry muffin.

"Here you go. Vegan bran." Eli handed the dark dense ball to Nate. "Did you? Are you suddenly available?" He leaned across the counter and leered at Kellan.

"Bring me bacon next time and we'll talk."

"Ha. Nate will fire me if I despoil his home with animal flesh."

A greasy egg-bacon-cheese sandwich sounded exactly right

to Nate's hangover.

"But this is allowed." Eli produced a bottle of KZ X-treme Cream Soda, and Nate had the top off and was knocking back the fizzy syrup before Eli could put the bottle on the counter.

"I thought KZ Cola fired your dad?" Kellan said. "How do they rate a pass on your enemies list?"

Eli's hair was too long to see whether his brows arched, but his light eyes grew wide as he stared at Nate. "They did? When?"

"Shut up, Kellan."

Kellan grinned. "My dad doesn't allow the old company's stuff in the house. No aiding and abetting the competition." He picked up the bottle and took a healthy swig. "I missed this stuff. Do they still make that tangerine-coconut?"

"Yeah," Eli said. He was so busy watching the morning show his corn muffin was untouched in front of him.

"Hey, Eli, what would you say if some big pop-rock star came out?" Kellan dropped his non sequitur into the mix.

"Oh my God, who do you know? Who is it? I wouldn't tell anyone, I swear, not even if my mouth was full of his dick." Eli held up his palm like he was taking an oath.

"I don't know of anyone, but I was just saying, what if. And what if it turned out that guy was only faking it, like he only did it to sell tickets for his tour or more CDs or whatever."

"I'd say he was an asshole."

A triumphant *ha* burst from Nate's lips and made his head ring.

"An asshole, but a smart asshole," Eli went on. "He knows being gay is cool."

"Ha," Kellan said back.

"Wouldn't that bother you personally?" Nate forced a lump

of muffin down his esophagus.

"Why?" Eli asked.

"Because we're a minority and those actions get magnified and affect us all."

Eli shrugged. "But the asshole would still be straight, so why would it matter?"

"Eli, man, I could totally kiss you right now," Kellan said.

"I'm in." Eli darted around the counter and jumped onto Kellan's lips.

Nate expected Kellan to push Eli away, but Kellan put his hand on Eli's cheek, and from where Nate was standing, the kiss was soft, and there was movement going on in there.

Nate really wished he'd gotten the hang of that repression thing, because then he would have been able to tell himself that the jolt to his stomach was from a vegan bran muffin on top of a gallon of water in a queasy hungover system and not jealousy. Kellan wasn't really his boyfriend any more than Eli was, so watching them kiss, even if it only lasted six and a half seconds, shouldn't have any effect on Nate. To give his budding belief in repression a little growth spurt, he applauded.

"Let's go, Eli. We're going to be late."

Eli licked his lips and winked at Kellan. "No, we're not." His grin vanished. "Oh shit, Nate. I was playing around. Are you really jealous?"

"He is," Kellan said. "He's always been really possessive. Never learned how to share."

"This is because I didn't let you ride the bike I got for my tenth birthday before I did."

"Oh my God, did you guys grow up together? That is the—"

"Say sweet and you are so fired," Nate warned.

Eli shut his mouth and grinned again.

"You." Nate pointed to Kellan. "Come with me." Nate led the way into the bathroom.

"Told you. Possessive," Kellan said to Eli. "Coming, baby."

"Okay." Nate shut the door behind Kellan and took a deep breath, trying to find his center or his chi or whatever the fuck he'd never been able to find in meditation because spending that much time alone in his head made him want to jump out of his skin.

Kellan leaned against the sink. "Yeah?"

Christ, there wasn't enough room in this bathroom for them both, wasn't enough room in the apartment, and sure as hell there wasn't enough room in Nate's life. Two months. He could do this. Revenge for the way Geoffrey screwed over his dad and a good deed for the city.

"Are you really pissed because I kissed Eli?" Kellan straightened from his slouch, face suddenly serious. "I didn't mean to fuck with your love life, man. If you want to get with him or—"

"No. I don't want Eli. I fucked him once but—"

"Really? Like fucked him fucked him?"

"Do you want a play-by-play?"

"Well, I don't exactly know what you guys do."

"You take a dick and you get it wet and then you put it someplace tight—"

"No, like how do you know who fucks who?"

Blood pulsed, heat beating in Nate's dick. "I don't think you're ready to find out."

"What's that, some kind of club secret?" Kellan leaned against the sink again, tugging the sweats away from his own half-hard cock.

Nate stared at Kellan's crotch until it made him shift again.

"You want to know because it's turning you on?"

"I like thinking of my dick in someplace tight."

"And you couldn't get any girls to let you go for the back door?"

Kellan grinned. "Maybe Eli will take pity on me instead. Was it good for you?"

"I thought you wanted us to pretend to be in love."

"Aw, don't be jealous, baby." Kellan reached for Nate's cheek.

Nate slapped his hand away. "Cut it out."

Kellan folded his arms. "So are you in?"

"As long as you want to stay out."

Kellan laughed. Not the mocking kind Nate was getting used to, but a soft helpless snort that tickled Nate's ears. "You turned out to be a funny guy, Nathan Gray."

And Kellan hadn't turned out to be quite as much of a dick as Nate had thought he would.

"I'm agreeing to do this, but there are some rules."

"You are just like my dad." Kellan rolled his eyes. If Kellan started sucking his teeth, Nate would be ready to live up to acting like Geoffrey and throw the brat out onto the street.

"No kissing in the apartment. No touching in the apartment. No walking around without clothes on. And you don't call me *baby*."

"What about out of the apartment? We've got to make it look good."

"You really think people are going to notice? You were only on that reality show for a month."

"You watched it?"

"No." Nate could lie—when it wasn't really a lie. He hadn't

watched *Get a Job* when it was on but had seen some online clips.

"Eli noticed."

"Fine. When other people are around, touching and kissing. But nothing too gropey."

"Gropey? Don't you write a sex-advice column?"

"It's more like a life-advice column. You know what I mean. No matter what you've seen, gay people don't have public sex any more than straight people do."

"You should. Maybe it would be fun. You're too tense, man."

"Well, maybe when there's someone around I want to have fun with, I will."

"Don't wait too long. If you want to know what bitter and old looks like, I can reintroduce you to my dad."

Nate shoved his way out of the bathroom. "Ready, Eli?" He picked up the soda and finished it off. Between the fluid, the sweet syrup in the soda and the Tylenol, he was starting to feel human.

"I was right." One corner of Eli's mouth lifted in a smirk as he looked from Nate to Kellan.

Nate was ready to ignore him, but Kellan had to ask. "About what?"

"Who got the I'm-sorry blowjob. Nate's—uh—pretty vocal, so I was sure it wasn't him."

Nate started to shove the smirking Eli through the door but turned in time to see Kellan's brows arch as he mouthed *Vocal, huh?* at him.

Maybe the paper should send Eli on an assignment—to West Virginia.

Chapter Nine

Working at a coffee shop didn't suck, Kellan decided. The manager, Yolanda, had him fill out some paperwork and then showed him some video about how to interact with customers. Brandi, one of the girls who worked there, brought him an awesome iced mocha with tons of extra syrup. He tried to pay more attention to the video than to Brandi's ass as she walked out of the office, but the job wasn't rocket science or anything.

The other girl Sandra was nice too, if not as friendly, and the guy Terrell hadn't seemed to make up his mind yet about whether he was going to like Kellan. They didn't let him make any drinks. He got stuff out of the pastry case, brought people sandwiches or their orders if they had something complicated and were sitting at a table. He cleaned off the tables and carried stuff back into the kitchen to load the dishwasher. He smiled, the customers smiled back. He could do this.

After about an hour he had to clean out the prep area, restock the stuff for the front, and that's when he started to get an ache at the back of his neck because the place was small, and he was always ducking down at the doorway. Then someone in the outside world must have made some announcement that the café had winning lottery numbers or something. All of a sudden there were about a hundred people in line. As he tried to navigate around the crowd with his tray full of dishes, Brandi looked up from where she was spreading cream cheese and peanut butter on a bagel and mouthed *Lunch.*

He wanted to check his phone to see the time, but Yolanda was yelling at him to bring up more bean sprouts. He couldn't get away from fucking beans—and the fact that these looked like little sperm to him didn't make him any more fond of the nasty things. As he unpacked the slimy-looking sprouts, he tried to think of something nicer: Brandi.

Curvy, blonde and working hard to get him to notice her. Exactly the type Kellan liked to flirt out of her clothes. As he dropped the container of bean sperm in the hole that Brandi pointed to, he ended up right next to Terrell. Instead of aiming a wink at Brandi, Kellan found himself wondering whether the ink on the light brown skin of Terrell's neck and the heavy piercings in his ears meant he was punk or gay. On the way back with the container of honey-walnut cream cheese, he found himself wondering if Terrell's full lips would be soft like Eli's or if the soul patch on his chin would feel different from Nate's fuller beard. It should have freaked him out, but when he looked at Brandi's lips and knew what they'd taste like, feel like under the shine of her lip gloss, his little soldier reported ready for action.

So one day of pretending to be gay hadn't actually made him switch teams. Which reminded him of that other time when he'd been confused about what side he was on, and too much thinking for one day was probably why as he lugged out a big container of egg salad, he crashed into Brandi with her arms full of clean plates.

Brandi managed to stay on her feet, but Kellan had tried to swerve and his foot slid on a slice of tomato. A banana peel couldn't have been slipperier. The egg-salad container hit the ground and puked out yellow bombs of gluey sulfur, two of the plates shattered, and all of it landed on Kellan who hit the ground first.

Brandi tipped her head to the side as she looked at him, recognition breaking across her face. She dropped the last of the plates. "That Kellan? Like Kellan and Kimmie on *Get a Job.*"

"Yeah."

"Eighty-six the egg salad," she yelled over her shoulder before helping him to his feet.

Kimmie, fiancée number two, was a model who'd been trying to break out in reality TV. Her agent got her a spot on a show where famous, rich, powerful and pretty people had to compete by doing all kinds of messy physical work, like mucking stable stalls and hosing down port-a-pots. It was set up so no matter what, the people on the show always ended up covered in crap. Pretty people getting dirty makes good TV, the agent had said. The producers had wanted both of them, so Kellan had gone along for a couple of episodes. It figured that covered in glops of egg salad and surrounded by broken plates would be the way he'd get recognized.

"Holy sh—crap. Is this another show?" Brandi lowered her voice to a whisper. "Are they filming us now?"

"No, I really needed a job."

"Whatever." Brandi sighed.

Wow. His dad and Nate weren't the only ones who could pull that you-disgust-me-Kellan face.

"No. I do need this job." He got back onto his knees and started loading pieces of dishes and scooping egg salad into the rubber dish bin she'd brought over. "I pissed my dad off, and he threw me out of the house." Kellan was good at lying, so when he told the truth, it was magic.

While they picked up the plates, Brandi pressed up against

him, her breasts rubbing along his arm. "What did you do?"

Kellan's little soldier knew what that tickle meant. Knew what the soft floral smell and the caress of a ponytail along his neck meant too, no matter how many times Kellan told him to stand at ease. There might be some officer fragging, but Kellan was going to have to say it. "I couldn't be what he wanted me to be. I needed to be honest."

"About what?"

The *I'm gay* bit got stuck, but he found an easier way to say it. "About being in love with Nate. My boyfriend."

"What?" Brandi jumped to her feet with the bin under her arm. "You can't be gay. You— What about Kimmie?"

"It wasn't real." Kellan stood to face her.

"I can't believe it."

"It's true. Nate and I have known each other forever. I just got tired of trying to fake it."

Her face softened in that way Kellan knew meant he was totally going to get exactly what he wanted, which was usually that same face rubbing sweet and slow over his dick before she wrapped her pink-glossed lips around the head, but this time he was pretty sure that was off the menu, damn it.

She put a sympathetic hand on his arm. "Wow. That must have been hard."

Oh, he wished she hadn't said hard, wished her hand wasn't warm on his bare skin. Kellan tried to think of something that would cool him down, hit on Nate's dark, challenging stare, and that didn't work at all.

"What?" Terrell stomped past them on his way to get fresh plates out of the rack. "You know what's hard? Doing the whole lunch shift alone while you're trying to get in his pants."

"He's gay."

Terrell looked at Kellan, who bit his lip and nodded.

"Yes." Terrell punched his fist in the air. "Sandra! You owe me your cut of the tips."

"No way." Sandra stepped back from the counter and peered into the kitchen.

Kellan shrugged, holding his hands open in apology.

"Are you asking where the mop is, Kellan?" Yolanda called back.

"Yes, ma'am."

She pointed and Kellan went to find it.

He'd had worse happen to him on the TV show, but Kellan didn't want to get the mop. He wanted to toss his apron in the trash and head right out the back door. It wasn't the mess— even though he still couldn't get the last bits of egg salad to let go of his hair. It wasn't because he'd disappointed his little soldier by ensuring that Brandi would never hit on him again. It was something he couldn't put his finger on, though his balls wanted to crawl up inside him at the thought of grabbing the mop and going on like nothing had ever happened.

But if he walked out, he could either grovel for his father or admit to Nate that he couldn't handle a single day on his own. Kellan got the mop.

There was a lull of about ten minutes after the first horde had been fed and recaffeinated before the second wave hit the door. The rush seemed easier this time. He didn't crash into everybody, and they all started singing along to some of the soft rock on the radio, so the time went faster.

"Ooo. Pretty mouth and a pretty voice," Terrell teased as he helped Kellan rebag one of the trash cans.

"God, Terrell, you're such a slut. He has a boyfriend." Brandi had her hands on her hips in that weird solidarity girls got about the possibility of guys cheating. They had one hell of a network, which made them tougher to ditch than the paparazzi.

"Now that is a crime. He's too pretty for that."

The teasing made it easy to play along, so Kellan dragged Terrell with him to the back door like he was about to have his way with him.

By three ten, Kellan knew he was going to make it. The café closed at three thirty, but only six customers came in after two, and Sandra and Kellan cleaned around the one guy reading a paper in the corner so that they'd be able to leave on time. Yolanda was in her office, and Brandi and Terrell were doing something complicated to the espresso machine, when Kellan spotted Eli walking past the front windows ahead of Nate and some woman.

Eli had a huge camera bag over his shoulder.

Brandi abandoned Terrell to the machine's growls and hisses and ran over to Kellan, waving her phone. "I'm sorry. Really. I didn't think it would be such a big deal."

"Huh?" Kellan glanced at her and then back at the trio coming into the café. Nate was wearing glasses. He hadn't been wearing any yesterday, so Kellan had figured Nate had either had that laser surgery or started wearing contacts. The frames were dark and squared off, completely different from the kind he'd worn as a kid, and they looked right on him. Maybe his eyes were dried out from his drinking last night, but he looked better in them than out of them. More Nate-like.

"Nothing ever happens in Baltimore, but here you were, so I emailed a friend with a pic, and she put it online and now—" Brandi was still talking, shoving her smartphone under his nose.

"What?" Kellan looked at the phone's screen. There was an image of him in his egg salad smeared apron, playfully steering Terrell toward the back door with an arm around his neck. But that wasn't all. The pic was on one of the big gossip sites with the headline *Unreality Star: Bad-Boy Brooks Likes Boys.*

"I hope I didn't make things worse. I didn't think it would get all blown up like that," Brandi apologized again.

"What would get all blown up?" Eli tried to get a good look as she waved her phone. Finally, he grabbed it from her hand. "Oh, fuck. We've been scooped. What happened?" He handed the phone off to Nate.

Nate glanced down than passed the phone back to Brandi with a quick apology. "Looks like you've been outed." Nate stared at Kellan, eyes unreadable behind those solid brown frames.

The espresso machine might have been spitting steam right into Kellan's ears to make them feel so full of noisy air he couldn't think straight. This was his plan. And it was working. But he kept remembering how fucking hard it had been to get those words out to Brandi—and he really didn't give a shit what she thought about him. It wasn't only his dad who was going to see this. Everybody. Everyone he'd known. Delia and Kimmie and Rainy would believe he'd been lying to them when he said he'd loved them, wanted to marry them. Even his mom, if she got news at the spa where she was spending the month to recover from her disappointment at losing another potential daughter-in-law—or more likely, the chance to plan a wedding showing off how rich they were.

And he was going to have to make them believe it or it all fell apart here.

Eli looked like he was about to make another dive for the phone.

"Calm down, Eli. We'll be the paper who has the in-depth story, and the bigger outlets will come to us to rerun it. Along with your photo credits." Nate's voice was calm but full of authority. He kept holding Kellan's gaze, fixing him to that spot, like Nate knew Kellan really wanted to run and stick his head under an ice-cold faucet and rinse away the blush that lit up his cheeks until they felt like they were smoking.

Nate had been living with this forever, this everybody knowing. Everybody thinking about what you did in bed.

"Excuse me. Maybe Kellan doesn't want to be in your story." Brandi stepped in front of him like her small body would shield him from evil reporters. "And you can't do it here without my manager's permission. Yolanda?" She raised her voice.

Her protectiveness was sweet, and Kellan felt bad about thinking of her as a walking blowjob.

Nate jerked his chin a fraction in Kellan's direction, like Nate was saying *Your move, man. What's the play?*

Kellan gave Brandi a smile. "This is Nate. My boyfriend." He leaned forward and kissed him.

Chapter Ten

Nate met Kellan halfway, mouth open enough to make it more than a casual peck. As his arm came around Nate's shoulders, Kellan's breath slipped quick and fast past Nate's lips. Nate put his hands on Kellan's cheeks, the heat of his embarrassment scalding Nate's palm. His action also shielded them for a second as their foreheads pressed together.

Where Nate's pinky grazed the edge of Kellan's neck he found cool sweat. This wasn't only embarrassment. It was starting to look like panic. "You okay?" Nate pitched the words so they were barely a murmur on Kellan's lips.

Nate felt Kellan's answer first in a tiny nod against his forehead, then Kellan stepped in until their bodies were tight together.

"Let's make it good," Kellan added, so low Nate felt the words more than heard them.

Nate returned the nod the same way, slid his hands to grip tight on the back of Kellan's neck and kissed the fuck out of him.

At first it was just a glide, moving from one lip to the other, soft tingling pressure while Eli's camera clicks circled around them in a quest for the best angle, the best lighting. Then Kellan's mouth softened, opened, invited Nate in. Something about Kellan Brooks's mouth melting under his made Nate the one who was finding it hard to breathe without gasping. Heat flared, snapped loose a hunger Nate had kept caged for as long as he could remember.

The kiss went from a calculated display of passion to wet and sloppy, Nate chasing Kellan's darting tongue into the spicy-slick warmth of his mouth. The hunger became open-mouthed desperation, a need that wouldn't back down. Kellan held on, hand in Nate's hair, one on his back and oh, Christ, Kellan's dick was hot and full against Nate's thigh.

That was it. Nate could steer Kellan right through the back door, slam him up against a dumpster and fuck into his dick until they both were raw and wet and limp, and still he wouldn't let go of Kellan's mouth.

It had nothing to do with the fuzzy teenage dream of Kellan loving him back, of them having a house somewhere, of them holding each other all night. It was this man, now, the hardness and the taste of him better than anything a thirteen-year-old could imagine. And worse than any torment his thirteen-year-old self had suffered. Because that had been a fantasy. The want howling and tearing at him now was all too real, and even less likely to be satisfied.

Kellan groaned, and whether that was part of the show or not, it made Nate harder than he'd ever been, dizzy with the loss of blood in his brain, which would explain why he kept right on kissing Kellan's mouth, rubbing his dick into Kellan's hip, fingers numbing from their clasp on Kellan's neck.

The only thing that spared Nate the abject humiliation of coming in his pants in front of a bunch of people was Jess, his feature writer, yelling, "Hey, Gray. There's something called a deadline that we lowly writers have to pay attention to so you dickheaded editors don't fire us."

Jess. The article. Right. The guy he was slowly peeling

away from wasn't his boyfriend, his lover, some wet dream come to life. It was Kellan. And Nate had fallen for another one of his schemes. None of this was real.

"Wow," the blonde girl with the phone said. "He really is gay."

"I second the wow," Terrell added, "but I already knew that."

Nate turned to Jess. "Okay. Let's get started."

"It's okay, baby," Kellan purred, rubbing his thumb over Nate's lips. "I missed you too."

Nate would have sworn that a man couldn't purr without sounding like a vampy caricature, but the deep rumble buzzed low in his ears, exactly like Yin's when she was settling onto his lap for a few hours of petting.

Being torn between smacking Kellan's hand away and sucking that thumb into his mouth kept Nate from doing either.

"So. Is there a place we can do this interview?" Jess said.

Yolanda came out of the back. "You know we close in fifteen minutes."

"I'll lock up," the blonde girl offered.

"I'll help," Terrell said, those two words carrying a load of innuendo. Nate always liked it when Terrell waited on him. He could turn an office run for coffee, bagels and cream cheese into lascivious pillow talk.

Nate took another step back from Kellan. "Here. I had an extra key made. I should probably head back over to the office."

"Sit down, Gray. You're both in the story." Jess pointed at a chair.

Nate hitched himself up on the window ledge next to the table. Kellan flipped a chair around and straddled it, flashing a grin so broad it carved deep dimples in his cheeks. The sight strained the leash Nate had put on the need to slam Kellan up against the nearest wall, until he realized the twinkle in those green eyes was for Jess. But the thick length outlined between denim-clad legs, who was that for?

"Why don't you start with when you first decided to come out?" Jess turned on a recorder and opened her laptop.

Nate was glad he hadn't had time to eat lunch because he'd have lost it as he listened to Kellan spin a story of how they'd always been close friends, but that his dad had been suspicious and tried to keep them apart. Kellan had wanted to live up to expectations but had kept missing Nate. Now nothing would come between them. They were a not-quite-as-tragic Romeo and Juliet.

Jess deftly spun the questions back to Kellan's history of engagements, about his trail of broken hearts. Kellan summoned the appropriate look of shame so easily Nate wondered why he hadn't stayed in acting.

"I was terrible to them. I think it was an internalized homophobia, you know? Like fear of what everyone would say. I tried to tell myself that if I could make the engagements work, I'd make everyone happier."

Kellan must have spent last night reading the books in Nate's apartment to come up with that internalized-homophobia line. It was dangerous to leave him alone.

"Well, what about other men? Have you been in relationships with other men?"

"No. I—" Kellan's gaze lowered, blush dark on his cheeks. He must have been able to fake that too. "It's really always been Nate."

"But you do find men attractive, right? You say you're gay."

Kellan looked at Nate like he was supposed to throw out a lifeline. Nate only gave him a smile. This was Kellan's fairy tale.

83

"It's kind of awkward with my boyfriend right here," Kellan said at last, gaze shifting away from Nate.

"I'm sure he doesn't mind." Jess was actually falling for it. Jess, who used to do most of their movie reviews, who sneered through all the emotional moments of even the most heart-tugging children's movies, was buying every lie from Kellan's lips in the name of romance.

"To me it's always been more about love than labels," Kellan said.

"So you still aren't comfortable with saying you're gay?"

"It's not like that. I'm in love with another man. If that makes me gay, I'm proud to say so. Proud to be with Nate."

It was fucking genius. If Kellan had said he was gay, that he'd turned overnight, no one would have believed him. But this, it was like he was reading off some script. He could have been a screenwriter too. Hell, from the way he'd gotten Nate to go along with him, Kellan could have been the old triple threat: starring, written and directed by.

"So what do you think about it, Nate?"

They were screwed now. Kellan had been right. Nate wasn't cut out for lying. Never saw a need to develop that skill. Kellan laughed a little, like he was nervous, but then he blew Nate a kiss.

Nate opened his mouth and surprised himself with the absolute truth. "It's killed me to see Kellan wasting his life all these years. I only want him to be happy."

Jess rolled her eyes and sighed. "Really? That's pathetic, Gray."

"What?" Nate drew himself up straighter and stopped swinging his legs. Jess bought all of Kellan's shit, but him she was going to question? Her boss?

"Could you at least give me a usable—and by that I mean something someone could read without gagging—quote for this print blowjob you're making me write?"

Kellan rolled his lips in, fighting a laugh.

Eli lowered his camera to reveal his smirk.

Nate sputtered. "Eli said you thought it would be a nice piece."

"Right, because it would be a great career move to turn down a suggestion from your boss." Jess stuck a pen between her teeth and tapped away on her keyboard.

"You're right. It wasn't a good idea to take advantage of the paper like this. We'll check with one of the other weeklies—"

"Forget about it. At least we'll still be the only paper in the city that isn't swooning over the Orioles winning ten in a row. Let's try something else. What do you have to say about the reaction of Geoffrey Brooks to his son's latest love interest?"

"I'll give you a quote on that." Nate swung off the sill. "Geoffrey Brooks can expect—"

Kellan reached up and grabbed Nate's arm, standing so they were holding hands. "My dad can go fuck himself."

Nate finally mastered the art of rationalization as he shepherded the article on Kellan's coming out through edits and layout to print. In fact, every comma in that week's edition received his personal attention as he stayed in the office as late as possible to avoid going back to his apartment—to Kellan. But then again if Nate knew that he was rationalizing his avoidance, did it still count as a rationalization? He would have asked Martin, the senior editor, if Martin hadn't left two hours ago at midnight.

The quiet office didn't give his brain much else to chew on

but the events of the day, one in particular.

There hadn't been any coercion in that kiss. Nothing to guilt about with Kellan's active—Jesus, firmly committed—participation. No. This time it was all about what Nate couldn't have. So maybe Kellan was curious. Some otherwise straight guys were. Maybe he'd be interested in a guy blowing him or fucking another guy, but it would be just another one of Kellan's stunts. And Nate couldn't be that guy. There was no way Nate could stand being nothing more than Kellan's trial run on the bendy track.

Nate sure as hell couldn't handle that when he got so stupidly worked up over a kiss. He wasn't fifteen anymore, but that hadn't stopped the uprising in his pants every time he thought about Kellan hard against him, mouth open, throat vibrating with a moan. And now Nate had another reason to stay here until long past everyone else shutting down and heading home. At least here he could jerk off in the bathroom in peace—rather than have to do it at home with Kellan in the apartment. Flushing his pipes should at least make him able to stand being in the same room with Kellan. Now he had to figure out how to sleep next to him.

Broad chest stretching out another of Nate's T-shirts, Kellan lay sprawled across most of the bed when Nate finally made it through the door at two. Tomorrow Nate could sleep in, unless there was an emergency with the printing and distribution. After he got out of the bathroom, he surveyed the landscape by the light from the streetlight on the corner and executed an acrobatic arch around Yin to find a spot on the mattress.

As soon as Nate got the sheet over him and his pillow precisely the way he wanted it, Kellan flopped an arm over

Nate's hips.

"Shove over, Kell." The déjà vu from those three words made Nate smile until an equally strong frisson of agony had him bolt up, feet on the floor. Because this wasn't one of those hundred times they'd been tucked together in Nate's bed as kids, when a shove from a hand or a hip meant nothing more than friendship. Now he was surrounded by the smell of Kellan's skin, the sound of his breath, drowning in the need to roll on top of Kellan and put way more into him than his tongue.

"What's wrong? Drunk again?" Kellan's voice sounded deeper than usual in the dark.

"I'm fine. Just thought of something about the paper."

Nate heard Kellan drop hard onto his back.

"Yeah, the paper." Kellan's laugh was more breath than sound. "At least you haven't cut yourself off from ever getting laid again. While every guy you were ever friends with is wondering if you take it up the ass."

"Christ, Kellan, then why the fuck did you do this?" Nate spun around to face him, moving so abruptly Yin took off to find a quieter spot. She paused by the kitchen island to level an evil glowing glare in his direction.

Kellan sat up and dragged a hand through his hair. "I don't know. I guess it seemed like a good idea. I mean, I still think it's a good idea, but it feels weird."

Nate turned back to face the window. "Yeah. Weird. I get that." A Kellan a lot hotter than anything Nate remembered, who he got to sleep next to and kiss but not really touch, was about as weird as it got.

Kellan laughed, an audible chuckle this time. "Maybe it wouldn't be so weird if I actually was doing what everyone's going to think I'm doing."

"What are you saying? You want to be doing it?" Nate turned on the bed so he could watch Kellan's face in the light from the street. Was Kellan trying to ask Nate for it?

Kellan shrugged.

Nate launched himself on top of Kellan, pinning him on his back with hands on his shoulders, and leaned close to his ear. "You want me to fuck you, is that it? You want my dick in your ass, Kellan?"

Kellan's lips curled in before he spoke. "I didn't say that." But Kellan didn't try to shove Nate off. Broad shoulders flinched under Nate's hands.

Nate wanted to scream in frustration. This was another one of Kellan's games, to get Nate to go far enough so that Kellan could laugh it off as a joke and make Nate the aggressor who took things too seriously.

"I might be doing this for my own reasons, but I'm not that much of a whore." Nate sat up, still straddling Kellan's hips, and lunged across to the end-table drawer. Tossing the lube and the dildo on Kellan's chest, Nate said, "Try it out and let me know what you think. Practice sucking it too. I'm not into virgins."

He swung off Kellan and stood up.

Kellan rolled onto his side facing Nate, picked up the dildo and tossed it at his feet. "Now I know why you've got one of those. You're such a self-righteous prick you're the only one good enough to fuck you."

Nate gaped at him, hands curling into fists. He'd never wanted to punch someone before in his life.

"That's right," Kellan went on. "You may not be whore enough to fuck me, but you're whore enough to fake a big gay love for revenge. Get off your high horse, Nathan. This is so much more about my dad than saving the city from some evil corporation."

"Do you know what it did to my dad? Did you hear what happened when old Geoffrey went public with the energy-drink formula he stole from my dad? KZ Cola threatened to put him in jail for industrial espionage and theft. We lost our house. Everything."

Kellan's face, pale against the shadows, grew dark as he flushed. "I didn't know all that."

"No. You were too busy at your new school, in your new mansion, to worry about that. Not that you even gave a shit about me then."

"I could try to fucking apologize again, but I don't know what the hell would be good enough for you. I'm sorry I wasn't born perfect. I'm sorry your life sucked. What was I supposed to do?"

"You were supposed to be there, Kellan." It was Nate's turn to shove the scar on his forearm under Kellan's nose. Nate kept his voice low and tight so it wouldn't break with the still-raw memory of that betrayal. "I never let you down. What happened to you?"

Nate was learning to read this older Kellan. The lip biting Kellan had done when he was anxious had become a quick pull in between his teeth, pushing it out to make his bottom lip fuller.

This time though, Kellan bit his lower lip so hard Nate thought there'd be blood. "I turned into a dick. Does that make you happy?"

"No."

Kellan glanced over at the clock on the table. "Shit. I'm supposed to be back at the café at six thirty." He ran a hand over his face. "Unless you're going to toss my ass on the street."

"No. I promised you could stay."

"Right. Noble Nate." Kellan stood up.

"Where are you going?"

"Newsflash: we ordinary people have to take a piss every once in a while."

If Nate climbed into bed now, maybe he could fall asleep before Kellan got out of the bathroom. One of the things about knowing someone for a long time was that you could always save the argument for later. That was, until you ran out of laters.

Chapter Eleven

Kellan headed off on his twenty-block walk to Manna Café with time to spare, relatively clean and dressed. Yesterday he'd taken advantage of the key Nate had handed him to let himself into the apartment and wash out his socks, shorts and shirt in the tub. His jeans were pretty bad and getting riper. He needed to find another pair or a place to wash them. There was no way he could fit into a pair of Nate's, and yesterday Yolanda had made the no-sweatpants-or-pajama-pants-at-work rule clear enough.

But not stinking up the place wasn't Kellan's only problem. Not even his biggest one. No, that went to figuring out why he'd been pretty close to having sex with Nate last night.

Was what he'd almost talked himself into some kind of flukey short in his wiring, or could he really play for either team?

If he took That Summer out of the equation, Kellan had been pretty happy scoring with girls. He liked their tits, their mouths, their softness, and he liked fucking them. When it came to the actual bumping-uglies part, he still wasn't exactly the kind of guy who got off just staring at a pussy, but once he had his tongue or finger or dick in one, he liked them a lot. Things took over and it was good. He was pretty sure he wouldn't get hard from nothing but staring at a dick either, so would things take over if he was with a guy? If he was with Nate?

And when he put That Summer back into the mix, his stomach got a lot more squirrelly and his nuts more shrivelly at the theory that maybe he could go there with any guy. But Nate wasn't any guy. And there was no shriveling and only the good kind of squirrelliness when he thought about Nate kissing him, Nate's body on top of his, Nate's hands holding Kellan's hips as—as what? That was about as far as he could go before his mind backed off like it was looking over the edge of a sheer cliff.

He cut through two alleys and over a fence to avoid going around the block to arrive at the café's back door by quarter after six. It was the first time he'd ever been early for anything in his life, but before he could take a deep breath of the rich morning smells from fresh roasting coffee beans, Brandi yanked him through the back door.

"Holy crap." Brandi tugged him through the kitchen. "Yolanda's having kittens. Terrell isn't on until ten and there's already a line." She pointed.

Kellan peered through the dark of the café to the glassed front where about ten girls were waiting, all of them looking at least one year under legal. Maybe there was a school close by.

Yolanda was pouring beans in the roaster and filling tanks. She did look ready to start snapping her fingers along with her directions the way she had yesterday during the lunch rush.

Yolanda grabbed the arm Brandi had freed and led Kellan behind the counter. "Kellan. Good. You can work the register this morning." Her Spanish accent was thicker today, maybe because she was in such a hurry. "The prices are all listed on the side there." She tapped her dark red fingernail on the laminated paper. "You take the money and make their change. The register will tell you how much. Sandra, show him. If there's a charge, Sandra will do it. You call her."

Sandra murmured and pointed at the keys, but other than figuring out what the drinks actually were when the customers got to him, it wasn't much different from hitting keys on a calculator.

"Of all days for the bakery truck to be late—" A beeping interrupted Yolanda, and she and Sandra rushed off to the kitchen.

They knew what they were doing, so Kellan stayed out of their way and tried to memorize the number and the items on the card. If he put it into a singsong rhythm, it wasn't that hard. The bakery items went into only two price categories— regular and special—and someone's tiny print gave examples of what each was underneath. He tapped his fingers lightly on the keys, getting the beats right. The only problem would be special orders, like extra shots of espresso or syrup. At least he didn't have to be the one making the half-skinny, half-soy, mocha and caramel, no-foam latte Kimmie had always demanded of the production assistants.

Yolanda unlocked the door and the customers streamed in. The first five girls were in matching school uniforms which made Kellan think his guess was right. They all ordered vanilla coffee milkshakes, which had Sandra and Brandi gritting their teeth because they required a lot of individual work. Each of them paid separately with a twenty which depleted Kellan's cash drawer, but then they each dropped two ones in the tip jar that read *Support Counter Intelligence* with a shy, "Thanks, Kellan."

It wasn't until after the third girl had tipped and stepped aside to murmur with her friends that Kellan realized he wasn't wearing a name tag. He kept eye contact with the next girl as he rang in her order and gave out her change. She blushed, but still thanked him and dropped money in the tip jar.

The other five girls only dropped their coin change, but they were less shy about eye contact and about using his name. A few people he guessed were regulars came in after the underage stalker parade, but the two groups of girls clustered at the end of the coffee bar and kept watching him.

Whether they wanted to get a look at someone who'd been on TV or to see a gay guy in his natural habitat, Kellan felt like he was in a zoo exhibit. Five more people came, the last two looking his way. Yolanda moved behind him muttering, "Hiring you as a favor for Nate is working better than his promise of free ad space for a week."

Kellan remembered Nate throwing around the word whore last night. He'd bargained for Kellan's job, which given Nate's over-exaggerated morals was kind of a shock, in a nice way. And it wasn't that Kellan minded the job. If people wanted to stare—well, it wasn't that different from his life before. They were just staring for another reason. He smiled back at the customers, turning up the charm, and more bills and change landed in the tip jar. Brandi gave him a friendly punch on his arm when someone tossed in a five.

By the time the coffee and pastry crowd had slowed to a trickle of people who stayed to sit and drink in front of laptops at the various tables, the huge jar was half-full and Kellan had only had to ask Sandra for help with the register once. Kellan couldn't remember ever getting something right like that the first time before. It was nice. The girls were nice. Yolanda was nice. And when Terrell strolled in and made a sexy whistle at the sight of the tip jar, his comments about Kellan shaking his ass for tips had them all laughing as Kellan acted it out.

Kellan wished the lunch crowd would start soon, because wiping down the empty tables gave him too much time to go back to wondering about where things stood with Nate, and if he wanted to actually find out—those things.

Nate would think it was a joke if Kellan flirted like Eli or Terrell, and Kellan couldn't see Nate being wowed with flowers or presents, not that Kellan had money to buy him something. It was weird to try to figure out how to get someone in bed with you when they were already there. Especially when you weren't sure what would happen and whether you wanted it to.

Kellan looked up from the table he was cleaning to see a black Town Car block the spot in front of the fire hydrant across the street. He already had a sick sensation in his stomach before he saw his dad's driver get out of the car.

Instead of opening the door for Geoffrey though, Shepherd kept walking, across the street and into the café. Kellan wiped the table again and waited.

"Mr. Brooks?" Shepherd held out a cell phone.

With a sigh, Kellan dropped the rag and put the phone to his ear. He knew one thing. There wouldn't be an apology on the other end of the phone.

"Kellan, please hold for your father," his dad's secretary said in the polite tone he'd heard so many times before his dad started screaming in his ear.

There was a longer pause than usual, then instead of screaming, his father's voice was pitched low and even. "What the hell do you think you're doing?"

"Looking for someone to make a man out of me, like you said."

Mission accomplished, Shepherd moved away to order coffee and give Kellan privacy. Most of the people who worked for Geoffrey were nice enough. It was his dad who was a dick.

"By pretending you're queer?"

"Did it look like I was faking it?"

His dad made a sound like he was in pain. Kellan would rather hear screaming.

"And you think that these latest theatrics of yours will make me want to have you under my roof again?"

"I don't care. Didn't you read the paper? See my message for you?"

"Yes, the Gray boy's paper. You realize he's only using you to strike at me."

"Right. Because he wasn't my best friend for most of my life."

"That was over a decade ago. You don't have any friends, Kellan. You've seen to that all by yourself, no matter how you may choose to blame or punish me."

Kellan slapped the rag against the table. "I'm punishing you?" His voice got high, almost cracked, and he was furious with himself—and with his fucking father for still being able to do this to him.

"You were told to stay out of the papers. The company is undertaking a major venture right now, and I don't have time for one of your hysterical episodes."

"You're calling me hysterical and you don't think I'm really gay?"

His father ignored that. "I will not have my son as the latest public exhibit of homosexuality. You will stop your most recent venture into drama and stay out of sight."

"Or what? You'll throw me out? Cut me off?"

"I wonder how eager your friend would be to help you out with your scheme if it affected the distribution of his newspaper."

"Try something else, Dad. If you were going to go after Nate, you'd have done it before this after all the stuff he's written about you."

"Perhaps. But everyone has their vulnerabilities. Like that little café Shepherd found you in. I'm out of patience, Kellan." His father disconnected.

There was no point in pushing the call-back button. Geoffrey Brooks always got the last word. Kellan stared out the window, though his eyes wouldn't quite focus. Finally, he took a deep breath and found Shepherd waiting patiently while he sipped his coffee. Kellan crossed over and handed the phone to Shepherd.

"You're a nice guy, Shep. But you work for a major fucking asshole."

Kellan walked through the kitchen and out the back door, stopping to lean against the sun-warmed bricks. No matter how many long, deep breaths he took, he still felt that break high up in his throat, and when he lifted his hand, he was surprised that it wasn't trembling.

"Kellan?"

He looked down at Brandi standing next to him.

Terrell stuck his head out of the door. "Told you he didn't smoke."

"Are you okay?" Brandi asked.

"The man's still not dealing with you coming out, right?" Terrell added.

That was one way to put it. "Right."

"Take your time," Brandi said and went back inside.

He'd worked there for one day—less than eight hours total—and they actually cared about him. Not the Kellan with money to burn or a reality TV star girlfriend, just him.

Now his dad would call someone at city hall, and Manna

Café would get hounded by the health inspector, or suddenly there'd be a water main that had to be replaced under the sidewalk in front, blocking the door. Kellan didn't know who owned the place, but he wasn't about to let Brandi and everyone else lose their jobs because of his dad.

He had to quit.

He found Yolanda in her office and explained what had happened, what he knew his father was capable of.

"Thank you, Kellan. If you need a recommendation anywhere, have them call me. I'll send a check for your hours to Nate at the paper."

"Thanks."

When he turned away from her tiny desk, he found Brandi and Terrell in the door.

"We cashed out the tip jar." Brandi handed him forty-eight dollars. "It was mostly for you anyway."

No way had that jar held that much money. They must have made up the rest from what they had on them. "Thanks, guys."

"Well, we are the people in your gayborhood." Terrell winked.

Sandra held up a bakery bag. "I packed you a lunch."

Kellan surprised them both by lifting her up in a big hug. Had he really only known them for a few hours?

Brandi hugged him next, and then Terrell used his hip to nudge her away and take her place.

"If you guys ever get tired of the same old thing..." Terrell whispered, adding to the offer with a slide of his hips.

Kellan laughed and thumped him on the back.

Terrell gave him a funny look as they separated. "I can see why Brandi was confused. That's some mixed-signal shit you got going there."

Kellan shrugged. "It's all kind of new to me."

Terrell tipped his head in a wordless whatever-you-say-man kind of way.

After Kellan left the café, he walked without any direction in mind. His shoulder blades itched with the idea that Shep or some other spy from his dad was stalking his heels, ready to lay down a threat against any place he went, but he never saw anyone when he turned back to look.

Sandra had stacked so much turkey, ham and cheese between the bagel slices that he had a hard time pressing the halves together as he ate, but after two hours of aimless wandering in Oldtown, he was hungry again. He tried not to think of the long trip back up as he headed toward the harbor and some fast food, but Mickey D prices were much more in line with his financial standing than any of the cafés in the fixed-up parts of the city.

He was about halfway back up when the clouds blew in, a quick, sudden, soaking shower. He'd been planning to find some place to get clothes, and when he saw the Goodwill store sign ahead, he knew he'd found something in his price range. He ducked in, shaking the rain out of his hair, wiping his face on his already-soaked sleeve.

The woman behind the counter looked him over and went back to thumbing through a magazine. A vicious combination of shame and guilt floated the burger in his stomach on waves of acid. He shouldn't be in here when other people needed it, and yet his cheeks flamed with the knowledge that he was one of those people. Needy people. People who had to buy a pack of underwear marked "irregular". What made underwear irregular? Did it have an extra leg hole?

The jeans—at least the ones that looked new—were between five and ten dollars. The ones that would fit him were all ten. He held them up to check the length and grabbed a few T-shirts and a pack of socks. Maybe when Yolanda sent the check, Kellan could afford some "regular" underwear.

He couldn't look the woman in the eye as he paid out most of the cash he had left. Everything in the store had a funny mold-stale-cigarette smell to it. Maybe he could find a laundromat on the way home and blow the rest of the five dollars in his pocket, but he would rather deal with the smell than give up the rest of his cash. He thought the people he used to hang out with were too focused on money. They should try living without it and see how much they thought about it then.

When he started up the stairs to Nate's apartment, a complaining simple rotation of guitar chords made him think someone, probably Nate, had a folk-music station on. But it was Nate, sitting on his sofa, making a painstaking effort at the basic GDC chords of what might have been "Margaritaville", except that he had trouble on the chorus.

Kellan kicked off his shoes. "You know, if you can play an F chord, you could play Bon Jovi's 'Wanted'." Nate had always liked Bon Jovi, though it was totally old when compared to Dave Matthews. That should have been an indicator of gayness, Kellan realized now. It had been more about crushing on a good-looking singer than the music.

Nate glanced up for a second. "I've tried but—"

"I could show you." Kellan tossed his shirt next to the basket where Nate kept his mail, remembered the wearing-clothes rule, rolled his eyes and pulled a T-shirt out of the bag. Despite being soaked, he was hot from his long walk back uphill.

"You can play?" Nate tried the chorus again, but the G to D

shift on "woman" got him every time. He stopped and turned the guitar over on his lap. "Wait. Why are you back? I thought you worked until closing."

This was another reason Kellan had spent all that time wandering around. Because Nate was probably not going to listen to much after *I quit*, and Kellan wasn't in the mood for a lecture. He'd had enough from his dad today.

He filled a glass of water from the tap and looked around for Yin. "I quit."

Nate put the guitar on the sofa, effectively blocking Kellan from having a seat anywhere but on the floor. "Why?"

Maybe Kellan had been hoping for a fight with someone, because the fact that Nate was waiting and listening pissed Kellan off as much as a sigh would have.

"My dad called."

"The café?"

"He sent his driver to track me down and hand off a cell phone."

Nate made a disgusted sound and shook his head.

"So my dad was having a fit about me being a freak show—he doesn't believe I'm actually gay by the way, even if I was kissing *that Gray boy*—and threatened to use one of his contacts in city hall to screw things up for the café."

"Why didn't he threaten the paper?"

"I think he'd have already come after you if he thought he could."

"Thanks for thinking of me."

"I didn't want the people there to lose their jobs, so I quit."

"How mature and unselfish of you."

"How stuck up and dickish of you to point that out. I

already have an asshole for a dad, man. Don't really need you to be one too."

Nate picked up his guitar and settled it back over his lap. His fingers squeaked as he shifted them on the frets, but he didn't strum it. "Are we done now? You pissed your father off; he noticed. When do you leave?"

"What happened to my two months?"

"What do you want, Kellan?"

"I thought we worked that out. You were letting me stay here until—"

"Until you could show your dad he couldn't control you." Nate's fingers squeaked over the strings again, making the hair on the back of Kellan's neck stand up.

"So you're going back on the deal."

"I think if you ask your mom, she'll let you have enough money to find a place to live and you can find a job." Nate looked up, eyes wide and dark behind the lenses of his glasses, and then quickly looked away, picking at a string.

The sound and the way Nate was chicken-shitting his way out of this pissed Kellan off.

He strode over and stood in front of Nate close enough that the neck of the guitar was an inch from Kellan's thigh. "I stuck with every one of your rules. And the point of this was to put pressure on my dad for his homophobia. So you're backing out and I want to know why."

A weird kind of energy held him there. Not only a maybe-I-want-sex thing or a c'mon-and-fight-me thing. Nate was right. Kellan had made his point, and he probably could get money out of his mom if he had to—if Nate would give him enough money to go find her. But as much as today—his dad, quitting, the rain and Goodwill—had sucked, Kellan didn't want to—

couldn't walk away.

Cutting Nate out of his life once had been hard. Doing it now would leave a bigger scab for his brain to pick at when things got too quiet. He wished Nate would get off that couch and shove him back, kiss him, maybe more. There was no way he could leave without knowing where this was going.

Chapter Twelve

Nate backed down again. "Okay. I guess we should find you another job then."

"Yeah," Kellan said without enthusiasm. "We can get right on it. Unless you want me to show you that F chord now?"

Things were weird enough without Kellan getting close enough to correct his fingering—on the frets. "Not right now." Nate put the guitar in its case but didn't shut it.

"Mind if I take a shower?"

"Go ahead." *Please. Get out of the range of temptation and get—naked and wet.*

As soon as the bathroom door closed behind Kellan, Nate dove for the desk drawer that held his cookies. The mouthful of thick frosting didn't do a thing to take his mind off what was in his bathtub. If Nate didn't stop trying to sublimate like this, the already too-soft edges on his hips from his desk job were going to turn into bona-fide love handles. Who knew that three days of Kellan's company could turn Nate into a textbook case for every neurosis he'd studied in Psych 101.

Not wanting to get caught with his hand in the cookie drawer, he went over to lean on the bathroom door and listen for the spray.

"*The Sun* is going to run some of the article we did

tomorrow, along with one of Eli's pictures," he called into the bathroom.

The water shut off. "He must be happy."

"Ecstatic. He's out celebrating."

"Did you want to go meet him?" Kellan opened the door.

The humidity from the shower escaped in a sweet-smelling cloud that made Nate want to lick his lips. Or maybe that was the chocolate frosting.

"Or we could go out tonight," Kellan added. "Didn't your paper have something about the DJ at The Arena?"

Nate jumped back. Kellan out at The Arena with all those guys grinding? Slap up another definition on the irrational-emotions wiki. Nate was jealous of a straight guy who wasn't his boyfriend and who would probably laugh at the idea of grinding with another guy. "No. Yes, but he's there for a week. Wait, do you want to go?"

Kellan shrugged. "It's hard following the clothes rule if you're standing right there and my stuff is on the counter."

"Right." Nate crossed over to where his computer was flashing through the series of *Rag* covers that made up his screen saver.

"What are you doing?"

"Trying to find you a job."

"At your paper?"

Nate turned and caught Kellan smoothing dark denim up over a pair of baggy Fruit of the Looms. Even that completely unsexy underwear made him have to turn back to the computer to hide a reaction.

"No. In the help-wanted ads."

"Good, because that would be weird."

Nate had barely managed to open a site when he heard a strum on the guitar.

"Mind if I fool around with this a little?"

It was a little late for permission. "Go ahead."

"Needs tuning."

Kellan plucked and tuned while Nate stared at the screen.

"I don't want to freak you out or anything, man, but I think someone stole your TV."

Nate didn't turn. "I don't have one. If there's something I want to see, I watch it on the computer."

"Seriously?" Kellan made a disgusted sound. "Do you have one of those Kill Your TV bumper stickers on your little scooter or something?"

Kellan was pushing for some kind of reaction. Nate wasn't going to give it to him. This was a game he remembered from when they were kids, though it hadn't felt so potentially explosive back then.

Kellan stopped the tuning and zipped through the opening riff of Metallica's "Enter Sandman", nailing all of the minor chords without the slightest hesitation. He stopped the hum and then played the opening to "Wanted Dead or Alive".

Nate was shocked and insanely envious. He turned around in his chair. "So when I asked if you could play..."

Kellan waved a hand. "Just something I picked up while I was wasting my life. I can mimic a lot of stuff I hear."

"Without the sheet music?"

"Usually. If it's not too weird. I can't read the rhythm, I have to hear it." Kellan stopped before the first verse and went through the opening again, every note annoyingly clear. "So you want me to show you the F chord now?"

"Okay." Nate stood.

Kellan handed off the guitar and then moved right in back of Nate, close enough that he could smell the soap from the shower.

Nate sidestepped. "Wouldn't it make more sense for you to be over here, where my fingers are on the board?"

"I can't do it from the side. I have to do it like I'm playing it."

Nate had seen this, rolled his eyes at this, in too many movies. Guy teaching girl to play pool or whatever activity the writers could think of to create some false sense of intimacy as he rubbed up against her ass.

Kellan didn't touch him anywhere but at his fingers though. "Relax." He grabbed Nate's first two fingers and shook them. "Here, do it on the couch so you don't have to worry about it slipping out of your hands."

With the guitar braced on Nate's legs, it was easier to let his fingers be moved around, but now Kellan pressed up against Nate's back, breath tickling Nate's neck.

"See, if you angle your finger back like this, it's not as hard." Kellan was right. Damn it. "Now go from—" Kellan's hand covered Nate's on the fretboard in a couple of quick motions, like he was remembering the chords. "You're going to need a shift from G to F, like this. Don't forget to angle back."

Nate made it through the first verse and a halting chorus, Kellan whispering the chords as he sang softly in Nate's ear.

"Good job." Kellan tapped his shoulder. "Want to try the opening?"

"I can't pick that fast."

"I'll pick, you do the fingering."

Eli would have been able to fire off a lewd comeback, something to get them all laughing, but this much of Kellan's attention was making Nate's brain short circuit on words. It was weird to be the one learning from Kellan.

"Ready?" Kellan asked, and then tapped Nate's hip to give him the rhythm before reaching around him for the strings.

It was perfect. Kellan made it easy and the music flowed by the second time through. Nate went into the first verse, and Kellan strummed while singing, thumb creating exactly the right resonance on the strings.

As Kellan increased the volume and speed for the second verse, his hand kept almost brushing the inside of Nate's thigh until even the most basic chord was too much for Nate's brain to communicate to his fingers.

"What?" Kellan didn't back off, resting his chin on Nate's shoulder.

Nate started to swing the guitar away and then realized he needed a cover for his lap.

"Oh." Kellan's cheek dimpled against Nate's with a smile. "Is that for Bon Jovi or me?"

"What?" *Move*, Nate told himself. *Put the guitar in its case and move before the conversation goes exactly where diving headfirst into the deep end of the cliché pool is leading.*

"The semi-woody in your jeans."

Nate wished the fact that Kellan was talking like a twelve-year-old was enough to back things off.

"Your hand kept going between my legs. Do I have to explain how dicks work to you?"

"So you want to fuck?"

The vision in his head of Kellan's head framed by the fragments of the guitar was tempting, but Nate put it into its case and shoved himself away, turning to face Kellan from the safety at the end of the couch. "Make up your mind, Kellan. Are you asking to have sex? With me?"

"I don't know. Maybe?"

"No."

"No what?"

"No. I'm not going to have sex with you."

Kellan had the balls to sit there and stick out his lower lip. "What's the big deal? We're just guys. It's not like one of us could get pregnant or—I mean you aren't, um, right?"

"The question is 'Are you positive?' and no I'm not. I don't have any STDs. But that's not the point."

"What's the point?"

"I don't want to have sex with you."

Kellan didn't seem upset by that. He lifted one corner of his mouth and stared steadily at Nate's crotch.

"Doesn't matter," Nate said. "Listen carefully. I don't care what you think you've figured out about wanting to try things with guys, it's not going to happen. I am not having sex with you." There. No more of this mixed-message bullshit. Clear communication, exactly the way he would have advised someone in his column. Of course, there was a reason why advice columnists got a lot of hate mail. They were morons doomed to spend their lives alone—with their overactive consciences. Nate pushed to his feet.

"Where are you going?"

"To get laid." Nate grabbed his wallet from his desk and headed for the door.

"Bring a little something back for me."

Nate held his middle finger up over his shoulder as he shut the door behind him.

Baltimore had a gay neighborhood and a good-sized community of guys who were good-looking and looking for it, but the options for finding them at four thirty on a Thursday afternoon were limited. Nate could have gone to the gym, which would have helped work off his sublimating sex with Berger cookies, but he hadn't grabbed a bag, and hanging out in the showers or at the juice bar felt a lot more awkward than a casual meet-up over free weights.

He hadn't ever been in a bathhouse, didn't have a Manhunt account. The fact was, until recently, sex had just happened. There'd been guys and they'd fucked, or they'd dated with fucking, or they'd dated and then fucked, and it hadn't been anything Nate had to work at.

He wished this sudden dry spell was something else he could blame Kellan for, but the truth was that it had been going on for longer than his seventy-two-hour recrudescence in Nate's life. Christ, had it only been three days?

Nate shouldn't have been surprised when Kellan found him at J.J.'s later. Nate had been nursing his second 7 and 7 for the last forty-five minutes when Kellan bumped shoulders with him as he hiked his ass onto the next barstool.

After grabbing Nate's glass and taking a swig, he made a face and ordered one of the microbrews they had on tap.

"How's the getting laid working out? Seems kind of dead in here."

"Staying power is one thing, but it doesn't take me two hours."

"So, not at all, huh?"

"Fuck you and shut up."

"I got a job."

"All by yourself?"

"Yes. Amazingly enough, I can operate a computer without people giving me directions. I'm working for the bakery that delivers to Manna Café. I'll be in the back dumping flour into mixing bowls, so my dad shouldn't care even if he finds out."

Nate swallowed a gulp of flat soda and whiskey as the bartender put Kellan's glass in front of him. Glancing over, Nate saw Kellan's cheeks start to blush as he realized he couldn't pay for the beer. With a sigh, Nate pulled another twenty from his wallet to put on the bar.

"Thanks," Kellan murmured into the thin head of foam. "I don't know if I'm ever going to be able to pay you back, but I'll try."

"Forget about it."

"Because you love having something to hold over me. Proof that you're the better man."

"It's not like that." It wasn't. Not exactly. He didn't care about money, other than having enough to pay his bills. But that wasn't what they were talking about.

"Whatever." Kellan downed half his beer in three gulps, and despite Nate's best effort, he couldn't help watch the way Kellan's throat worked, the movement of the muscles and tendons under the warm skin he was trying not to think about tasting.

The bartender was down at the other end of the bar, watching the news, but Kellan still pitched his voice so low Nate had to lean in to hear him.

"So you were right. I probably would freak out if you—if I got what I was asking for. But I've never liked getting no for an answer."

This was good news. So why did Nate feel like he'd swallowed all the ice cubes along with his last sip?

"It's no big deal. I know you're not gay or bi or whatever." Nate managed a half smile. "There's nothing wrong with being straight."

"Funny. Yeah, well, you were right about me freaking out back then too, and I'm sorry about that."

"It's fine." Nate wasn't lying. Somehow it didn't bother him as much anymore, and it wasn't only from Kellan's half-assed apology.

"So, can we call a truce?"

"Sure." Nate offered his hand.

Kellan grinned and used the handshake to pull Nate close but didn't kiss him. "Thanks, man. I did kind of miss you, you know."

Chapter Thirteen

Not only was Kellan great at lying, he also had no problem reneging on a promise. There wasn't going to be a truce. Nate had seen to that. If there was one thing Kellan couldn't handle, it was being told no. He knew it was childish and stupid, but telling him no was like waving a red flag in front of a bull. It sent him charging after whatever he'd been told he couldn't have.

And Nate had just waved Kellan's favorite red flag. Kellan hadn't been really sure he wanted to go there with Nate until Nate told him he couldn't. He'd made a career of convincing girls who swore they wouldn't have sex with him to be ready and willing in his bed.

He was going to have to be extra sneaky, though. Nate was smart, and this game had a whole other set of rules that Kellan hadn't figured out yet. Besides flowers and presents being out, he didn't think Nate was going to give it up for attention and compliments.

He gave it two nights, and then waited until he heard Nate make a sigh like he was drifting into deeper sleep. With his back toward Nate, Kellan made a little flop, dropping his shoulder and upper arm along Nate's chest. Nate gave another noisy breath, a contented sound. Kellan lowered more of his shoulder onto Nate, more contact and warmth, but no skin.

Damn, Kellan should have tried this without a shirt on.

He shifted until his forearm rested along the bristles under Nate's jaw, thumb knuckle in perfect position to provide a tiny massage to the soft skin behind Nate's ear.

Nate's breath hitched for a second. Kellan froze.

The "accidental" contact could be blamed as normal sleep motion. He'd use the excuse that he thought he was petting Yin if Nate asked what he was doing. Then Nate took a deep breath, and Kellan went back to moving his knuckle, circling with light pressure.

As seductions went, it wasn't particularly effective, wasn't doing much to raise Kellan's temperature—or anything else for that matter—but he liked doing it. Maybe because he was getting away with it, or maybe because Nate's breath came so slow and even, and resting weight on that warm hard body was good. Kellan fell asleep just like that.

The next night he skipped the T-shirt, complaining about the heat.

"It's been hotter," Nate said, looking anywhere but at Kellan's chest.

"I don't know. Maybe it's being around all those ovens all morning. I'm hot all the time now." Working at the bakery was nowhere near as fun as working at the café. Kellan usually worked alone, in the back, doing the big batches of cake batter and/or dough that would get turned into something special up front by the real bakers.

"Fine." Nate stripped off his shirt.

"Why are you taking off your shirt if I'm hot?"

Nate shrugged. "I hate sleeping in a shirt."

Nate had been sticking to that wearing-clothes rule like there was some kind of fine he'd have to pay. Of course, Kellan had to be at the bakery hours before Nate got up, so he might have missed some opportunities to gawk.

If someone had asked Kellan what he'd be looking at on a bare-chested guy he maybe-almost-definitely wanted to have sex with, after spitting out "Seriously?" and "Just hypothetically, right?", Kellan would have said the other guy's pecs. He thought he'd be checking out the definition, the nipples, the width, but instead, the dark, soft-looking hair on Nate's body sent Kellan's gaze directly to that path from navel to waistband, a spot that made Kellan want to touch or even taste because something about that trail of hair had Kellan's throat working and his balls tingling. It was what he couldn't see that was making him nuts.

Yeah, there'd been that awkward blowjob thing a week ago, but other than thinking *this thick thing is choking me*, Kellan hadn't paid too much attention to Nate's dick. Now he really wanted to see it. Touch it, definitely. Maybe try licking or sucking it again.

As Kellan stared, the bulge under the navy boxer briefs moved a little, as if Nate's dick could read Kellan's mind. Nate sat on the edge of the bed with his back to Kellan, so he stared at that instead, at the muscles under the skin, the line of his spine, the dip right before Nate's ass. That looked like a lickable spot too.

Kellan was too tired to wait for Nate to fall asleep tonight. He edged up against him until they were back to back, butt to butt.

"Kellan."

"Yeah?" His throat was a little dry.

"I thought you said you were hot."

"My front's hot. My back's cold." Kellan waited to see if Nate would roll away and tell him to find a blanket or put a shirt on, but Nate simply dragged the sheet from their hips to their shoulders and didn't say another word.

The bakery job wasn't much fun, but Kellan didn't deliberately mess with the batter to get himself fired. The thing was, he'd heard a woman out front complaining about the height of the sheet cake she'd picked up for her son's confirmation. So he did a little math and decided an extra half a cup of baking powder in the batter would give the bakery the fluffiest, tallest cakes in the city. And maybe he'd be a hero.

But the batter tasted funny, kind of metallic, after that, so Kellan put in more vanilla, and then more sugar, and then it looked too syrupy so he added a few more eggs. Now it looked the same and didn't taste all that strange so it would probably be all right. He wasn't sure how much of everything he'd added at the end, but he knew he could repeat the success when the baker asked him about it.

He filled the sheet pans exactly to the right line and shoved them in the ovens.

If it had only been the five sheet cakes, they might not have fired him. And probably wouldn't have said all that stuff in Hungarian or Polish or whatever it was they'd chased him off with. But Kellan's special cakes had exploded in the ovens, their dramatic death also obliterating six pies, eight trays of cookies and twelve nut-bread loaves. The smell was indescribable.

They didn't offer to mail him a check.

It was only seven when he walked to the bus stop. Most people hadn't even gotten up for work yet, and Kellan had already lost his second job.

The bus doors hissed open, but the driver put up his hand

to tell Kellan to wait. The bus tipped toward the sidewalk and a tiny old man with a cane made his laborious way down the stairs. Kellan wanted to help him, hell, he probably could have picked him up and carried him down the block, but the man seemed very intent on his shuffling path. A gust of wind made him tip a bit as he stepped onto the sidewalk, and the backpack he was carrying slid sideways. Kellan managed to save the man from falling, but the backpack went into the gutter under the bus. As Kellan retrieved it, the bus pulled away from the sidewalk.

It seemed like such a perfect exclamation point on his shitastic day that Kellan didn't bother to curse the driver out.

"That wasn't very nice," the old man said.

"Hey, man, I was only trying to help you."

"No, the bus driver."

Kellan was about to hand the backpack to the man, but wow, the sucker was heavy. "Jeez, dude, what you got in here?"

"Coffee, for one thing. The stuff at the center tastes like piss."

If the man hadn't been so tiny and old, Kellan would have accompanied his laugh with a slap on the guy's back.

"What center? I'll carry this for you."

The man pointed up the side street to where a sign read Barclay Center Rehabilitation Services. Since the old dude didn't look like one of those teen actresses strung out on coke, it must have been some other kind of rehab.

"Thanks, son. I'm Frank." He offered a soft, wrinkled hand.

Kellan shook it, offering his own name in return.

"Let's go, Colin."

Kellan shrugged and followed Frank. He was forced to take halting baby steps so as to not rush by him and spent the walk asking Frank what else was in his backpack.

"Cookies. Books. A spare pair of glasses. Change of pants."

"Whoa, man. How long are you going for?"

"Just the day. Hate to be unprepared. That philosophy has taken care of me for ninety-two years, and I'm not changing it now."

"Ninety-two? Wow."

"There's no secret to it, son. You get up every morning then life happens to you. You just have to have the right stuff to get through it."

"Yeah. Things do seem to happen to me a lot."

"Hmph. You smell like burnt cinnamon toast."

"That would be one of the things."

The woman at the front desk greeted Frank warmly and smiled at Kellan.

"Who's your friend today, Frank?"

"Colin, say hello to Miss B."

"Hello, Miss B."

Frank stepped into a room labeled Adult Day Care. No one seemed to mind, so Kellan followed him in.

"What are your plans today, Colin?" Frank eased himself into a chair at one of the tables.

"Didn't really have any. I just got fired."

"Good. No point going through life smelling like burnt cinnamon toast. Have a seat. Mary's never here on Wednesdays. She has a group that goes to a casino."

Adult Day Care. Kellan had a feeling Nate would think it was a perfect place for Kellan to be—with or without getting all the facts about his experiments at the bakery. It sure beat having to go back to Nate's hot and tiny apartment.

The place filled up, and at eight they started bringing around some breakfast trays. Frank poked at his French toast, then shared his coffee from his thermos and one of the cookies from his bag with Kellan. After breakfast, someone led a crafts class, making frames with dried flowers or pieces of old jewelry. Frank's fingers were still pretty nimble, so Kellan walked around and helped some of the other old people, picking up glue sticks that rolled away, pressing the decorations onto the cardboard.

Some of the people smelled a little funky, but it still beat working in the back at the bakery. People talked to him and smiled at him, and one old lady pinched his cheeks. When he came back, Frank told Kellan to stick around until they played cards at three o'clock, threatening to clean out Kellan's pockets at pinochle. That wouldn't take much. Kellan had enough for bus fare and an off-brand soda on him.

After lunch, a guy came in with a bunch of instrument cases. The singalong really perked up the crowd. The guy was better at keyboards, but he used the guitar occasionally. While he was leading "Take Me Out to the Ballgame", Kellan waited for a nod before picking up the man's guitar and strumming along. He threw in a "Shave and a Haircut" at the end and got a lot of laughs.

The music guy asked if Kellan could play Elvis's "Hound Dog" and they got everyone clapping. Kellan walked around the tables, winking, flinging his head back and doing some tame hip shaking.

Kellan couldn't wait to share his news with Nate, but the apartment was empty. Nate should have been home already, his late night had been Tuesday, the night they sent the paper off to the printer. Kellan plucked Nate's guitar out of the closet, and when the soft strumming made Yin come to sit next to him and purr along, Kellan told her about it.

"Guess what? And I did it all by myself. What's that? I got myself a good job."

"What kind of job?"

Kellan looked up to see Nate shut the door and kick off his shoes.

"Playing the guitar."

"On street corners?"

"No, at rehab centers. This guy put me in touch with a recreational therapist. And their usual guitarist needs the other kind of rehab, so I'm going to be going around the city to play for people in old folks' homes and trauma rehab centers and stuff like that."

Nate looking that surprised made Kellan wish he'd stuck to simply telling Yin about it. Provided he rubbed her belly and kept her bowl full, she didn't think he was too much of an incompetent moron to find his own job.

"Sounds good. Good for you."

Kellan couldn't figure out why it didn't sound good for Nate. "I get picked up at nine in the morning, so you don't have to worry about bus fare or anything."

"What about the bakery? Did you give notice?"

"Kind of."

Nate waited.

"I got fired. I was only trying to help."

Nate smiled, like the idea of Kellan screwing up restored the world to the way it ought to be.

"I feel like going out to eat. You want to celebrate your new job?" Nate pulled off his boots and headed for the shower.

"Do you eat in places that serve meat?"

"Sometimes."

"I'm in. I've got a twenty from the guy I worked with today."

"Keep it. It's on me."

Chapter Fourteen

At first Nate didn't know why Kellan's new job irritated him so much, but when his newfound skill at repression wore off, Nate figured it out. It only took a week to get used to having Kellan back in his life. As time went on, it became frighteningly close to one of Nate's preteen dreams of their future together, living together, sleeping together, with the scary sex stuff fuzzed out like bad reception. Now if Kellan didn't need Nate's help anymore, his friend would disappear, just when Nate remembered how much fun he was to be around.

It wasn't just their shared history either. Over the next month, Kellan gave such sexy and funny guitar lessons that Nate not only managed to get the F chord but A minor and two other barre chords with Kellan's patient help. Nate was getting used to having someone there besides Quan Yin to talk to when he came home.

He wasn't completely unaware of Kellan's pretend-to-be-sleeping cuddling either. After all, it was the most tried and true minimal rejection path to finding out if he was into you too, though what Kellan thought he was finding out Nate didn't know. He did know that for once in his life he'd decided to simply enjoy something because it felt good. And it did. Kellan played with Nate's hair, stroked the skin behind his ear, and rested a solid, heavy warmth on his shoulder, chest or back. It would have to have been a lot hotter in the apartment for Nate to shove Kellan away at night.

That month was a perfect amount of time to really get used to having Kellan there, and then Nate came home to the news that Geoffrey Brooks had sent his driver to pick up his son.

"Shep was waiting at the corner telling me my father wanted to see me. He actually expected me to get in the car just like that because the great Geoffrey demanded an audience."

Resisting the urge to throw his keys and a fist into the wall, Nate gently put them both into the bowl on the ledge. "What did you tell him?"

"I told him I had plans. Shep had to get on the phone and arrange a meeting. He's picking me up at five thirty tomorrow."

"In the morning?" When his chest squeezed tight, Nate had the horrible realization that not only had he mastered repression, but had achieved the absolute cliché of having his heart skip a beat at terrible news.

"No. I'm not getting up that early for Geoffrey, and we're hitting three centers tomorrow, including Marisol's."

Kellan had told him all about the teenager who had lost a big chunk of her brain in a car accident. She could walk and recognize people, but a huge part of her memory was gone, and so far she could only sing to communicate. Kellan and the music therapist worked extra hours with her and her family.

"Right." But after that? Kellan's stunt of playing gay might not have brought Geoffrey to his knees the way Kellan had hoped, but Geoffrey was too smart a man not to see the changes this month had made in his son. Kellan would be going back to his old life. What had Nate told Jess in that interview almost a month ago? *I only want him to be happy.* It was still the truth. No matter what, Nate was glad of the chance to have fixed up their friendship.

"So, are you coming in or going back out?"

"Huh?" Nate looked down to where his hand was still clenched around the keys in the bowl. "Yeah. Let's go out. The place across from J.J.'s has the best burgers in town."

"And I'm supposed to take your vegetarian word for that?" Kellan followed him down the stairs.

"Hey, I might be a vegetarian, but I know my meat." Nate turned and forced a wink.

"Holy shit, Nate. You made a dirty joke. Are you feeling okay?"

"I'm weak with hunger. Let's ride."

Kellan watched from five steps up as Nate dragged out the scooter. The way Kellan's stare moved over him made Nate feel like he was actually wearing the leather jacket and boots that went with that kind of statement.

Kellan nodded as if he liked what he saw. "I have got to get you an actual bike."

And that sealed it. No matter what Kellan might say about it, when his father offered, Kellan was going back to the life where he could buy someone a Vespa or a Kawasaki crotch rocket as easily as buying someone a coffee.

One thing about Kellan never changed. He flirted with everyone, male or female, from the cute busboy who brought them drinks, to the waitress who took their orders, to Nate. Maybe because Nate knew the game was over, he let himself flirt back.

He ordered a veggie burger covered in cheese and toppings, letting the sauce drip down to his wrist so he could lick it off while looking up at Kellan. When Kellan smiled with ketchup at the corner of his mouth, Nate leaned over close enough to lick it but only wiped it with his thumb.

It might have been wishful thinking, but Kellan's voice sounded a little hoarse when he said, "If you deep throat the pickle, I think half the guys in here are going to ask for your number."

"And the other half will wish they did."

"Wow." Kellan took a gulp out of Nate's glass. "I had to be sure you were only drinking club soda. What happens when you really cut loose?"

"Guess you'll have to keep wondering."

"You think so?" Kellan put a French fry in his mouth and pulled it out, slowly sucking off the ketchup.

Nate used a hand on his thigh to tug his inseam off his suddenly too-sensitive dick.

Kellan grinned like he knew exactly what Nate was doing. Nate licked his lips and was treated to the sight of Kellan's green eyes getting darker as the pupils widened.

"I think I know what I want for dessert," Nate said, stealing a fry from Kellan's plate.

When Kellan leaned forward, Nate told himself Kellan was covering his own need to adjust the pressure inside his jeans. "I thought since you ordered a salad instead of fries you'd be too worried about working it off to have dessert."

"Lots of ways to work it off. Even this late."

"Yeah, like what?" Kellan moved closer.

"I don't know." Nate sat back. "Going for a walk. Dancing." He was the one who got to wear the smirk this time.

"How come we've never gone out to any of the bars?" Kellan sat back as the waitress came to clear their dishes. "Afraid some hunky piece of ass will steal me away?"

"We've been to J.J.'s."

"I've found you there twice. It doesn't count."

They both turned down dessert when the waitress asked, and Nate paid the check.

"Do you want to go to one of the dance clubs?" Nate pressed back against the railing to get out of the way of a couple coming up the marble steps into the restaurant.

Kellan pushed forward when the couple had gone by. "Maybe another night. I want to be sharp for my meeting tomorrow. Let's go home."

Nate's chest did that squeeze thing again, this time pinching up in his throat with a sting that would have brought tears to his eyes if he wasn't so pissed at himself for getting caught up in his juvenile fantasy.

They didn't have a home together. And even if Kellan was a little or a lot bi-curious, he wasn't gay. Tomorrow he'd be a happy, wealthy heterosexual once more.

The scooter didn't roar like a Harley, but its puttering and the way they had to sit made it hard to talk as they went back through Oldtown to Butcher's Hill. But conversation didn't start up again when they were back in the apartment. Kellan sat on the couch and played the guitar while Nate worked on his columns.

It wasn't really goodbye. Nate knew he could trust Kellan to come through on his promise about the information. That was a chance to see him again. And Kellan would say he'd keep in touch, and Nate would get some emails and texts once Kellan had a phone again. But they'd taper off. At least it wouldn't be like it had been last time, when Kellan had gone from feeling like a part of Nate to being a cruel stranger. There'd be that all-important closure.

When they pulled out the sofa bed and climbed in, Nate should have known what was coming. After the flirting and the awkward silence, Kellan wouldn't be able to resist. Tonight it was a sigh and a wriggle against Nate's side. Neither of them had worn a shirt to bed since Kellan made his point about the heat, and Nate wouldn't use an ozone-depleting air conditioner until it was full summer. Nate kept his breathing even and glanced over. Kellan's eyes were shut, face relaxed. Nate was ready to let things go, but Kellan reached out and teased a curl of hair right next to Nate's nipple, and that was it.

Nate grabbed Kellan's wrist, fingers as tight as he could make them.

"Nate?" Kellan was still clinging to the whole I-was-asleep facade. He'd pitched his voice low, but it wasn't very effective with how quick his breathing was. "Um, sorry. I thought it was Yin."

"Bullshit." Without releasing Kellan's wrist, Nate got hold of the other one and pinned them over Kellan's head as Nate rolled on top.

Kellan tried a smile, but he couldn't seem to make it work. He licked his lips, and Nate ground his hips against Kellan's and kissed him hard.

Kellan didn't fight him, but he didn't kiss back, only left his lips parted enough to let Nate's tongue slide in. He teased the inside of the lips he'd been bruising, and Kellan's legs dropped open around Nate's. He worked his hips in tight jerks and then a long slide, angling to make his cock stroke next to Kellan's. Kellan's nipples got stiff enough to catch in the hair on Nate's chest, but it was the way Kellan groaned into Nate's mouth at the exact second that Nate felt the answering hardness against his dick that made Nate lose his mind.

They were moving together, a sheen of sweat on their chests, cotton pulling and tugging on their cocks. Nate wanted that last barrier gone, but—

He let go of Kellan's wrists and lifted his head.

Kellan bucked against him. "Fucking finish it." He grabbed Nate's shoulders. "Don't pussy out now."

Nate pressed himself up and got his hands on the waistband of Kellan's briefs. "Lift up and kick 'em off."

Kellan cooperated enough that Nate felt the damp—Christ, that was more than sweat—cotton slip down next to his calf. Nate would have ripped his own in half but just shoving them under his balls was enough. That first brush of hard, silky skin sent a shudder down Nate's spine and brought his balls up tight. He was so desperate to remember how to move his diaphragm that he almost missed the look of surprise on Kellan's face.

"So what do you think? You like cock? Like it hard against yours?"

"Shut up and get us off, Gray."

"Oh I will." This was his world Kellan was playing in now, and Nate had never had any complaints. Thinking about whose dick was riding hot and slick next to his made his hips work faster, made the friction so much sweeter.

He held Kellan's head between his hands and kissed him. "Yeah. You like it. You're gonna come so hard..."

Kellan yanked Nate's head down and held him for a kiss. It might have been to shut Nate up, but the way Kellan's tongue scraped over his, the moans leaking between their lips, told Nate Kellan was more worried about what would come out of his own mouth.

Kellan grabbed Nate's ass, squeezed and drove Nate harder against him. Nate shifted so the base of his cock gave Kellan's balls a rub, and Kellan's head fell back off the side of the mattress. His hips fucked back, fingers digging in hard as he panted, "C'mon. C'mon."

Nate bent his head and sucked hard on Kellan's nipple,

and Kellan's big body went still and tight before his hips moved in quick jerks and his dick spat wet and warm between their bellies. Nate worked his nipple until the panting and the motion slowed, until he heard Kellan take a gulp of air.

Nate started to lift his hips. He'd throw Kellan a towel and finish himself in his hand in the shower, giving Kellan time to freak out and get the spunk off him—maybe time enough to fall asleep.

Hands spread across Nate's ass, Kellan slammed Nate back down.

"No. Finish, damn it."

The growl in Kellan's voice rushed pressure from the hands on Nate's ass, to his balls, to his cock. Nate shifted up, aiming his dick for the groove on Kellan's hipbone. So fucking close and he didn't want to come, didn't want it to be over when he was looking down at those eyes glittering in the dark, the flash of teeth as Kellan bit his lip and urged Nate harder.

Kellan lunged up and nipped at Nate's neck, catching a tiny bit of skin right over his throat with a sweet spark of pain. He moved his lips to Nate's jaw, sucking, using his teeth.

"Don't leave a—fuck." It tore through him hard and quick, no way to back off and make it last. Nothing to stop those perfect spasms of pleasure breaking through him, firing off arcs of come from his dick until he was dry and his balls were still trying to work up one more shot. He caught himself on his arms before he fell against Kellan's chest.

"What? Do I have bad breath all of a sudden?"

"No." Nate slid off and sat on the edge of the mattress, rubbing his jaw. "You'd better not have left a hickey."

"What's the problem? Everyone where you work knows I'm crazy for you."

"Right." Nate pulled his underwear off the rest of the way and wiped at the come on his dick, in his pubes, on his belly. "Do you want to get cleaned up first?"

"Is that the way it works? You get each other off and then take turns scrubbing off jizz?"

Nate felt like he'd run straight up from the harbor, exhaustion sparking and shuddering in his muscles, twisting his gut with nausea. He wasn't in any shape to take on another one of Kellan's challenges.

"No." He turned and gestured between them. "That's how *this* works. Unless you want to lick it off."

"The way you're acting you'd probably bite it off. Don't you get mellow and happy after you come?"

"You want to cuddle?"

"Guess not." Kellan rolled off the bed and went into the bathroom, shutting the door quietly behind him.

Chapter Fifteen

Kellan spent about eight minutes in the bathroom, three cleaning up and the other five wrapping his head around the fact that what he was cleaning up was his come mixed with Nate's because they'd kind of had sex together. *So you had gay sex*, he said in his head as he looked at himself in the mirror. *And you really liked it.*

It had been a lot rougher than he'd thought it would be, which he liked, but then again, he'd never had that kind of sex with a girl, at least not since he'd convinced any of them to take their pants off.

So would he like it with another guy not Nate? He only really knew Eli. He couldn't see doing it face-to-face like that with Eli, maybe if he was facedown and Kellan put his dick in the crack of Eli's ass? That made his balls try to stir shit up again. So maybe anything could get him horny. No surprise there. He'd fuck until his dick was raw any day.

At the moment, Kellan was going to have to come down on the side of being bi. He whispered it at the mirror. *I'm bi.* And that was all right so far. Or it would be all right if the actually gay guy Kellan had had sex with wasn't the one freaking out and acting like a dick. He would have thought Nate might show a little concern about what Kellan was thinking, about whether he was freaking out.

But when he got out of the bathroom, though it had only been eight minutes, Nate was in bed curled up on his side.

Kellan tried to burn a hole in Nate's back with a glare and didn't get so much as a twitch. Then he turned on some soft needy eyes, and Nate still didn't move.

"I'm the one who should be freaked out, you know, dude." Kellan climbed in and lay on his back, arms folded across his chest.

Nate didn't say anything.

"Is this some kind of payback for me being a dick to you in high school?"

"No," Nate said, without turning over.

"What is it then?"

"It was sex. You wanted to know what it was like. Now you do."

Now Kellan knew, but now he also had a whole shitload of fresh questions. One new piece of info was that Nate was a different person when he was—fucking. There was probably another word for what they'd done, but fucking was close enough.

"Is that what happens most of the time? Is it like that usually? Or blowjobs? Or do you usually do the butt thing?"

"Sex for gay men is a lot of different things—like it is for anyone who isn't convinced penis-in-vagina penetration is the ultimate expression of human sexuality."

Now Nate sounded like one of his columns. Kellan had read some back issues online.

"Hey Gray, I've been reading your column for a long time and I hope you can help me."

Nate shifted but didn't roll over.

"I always thought I was straight, but there's this guy I've

been friends with for years, and we just had sex for the first time. He seemed really into it when we did it, but now he won't talk to me or even look at me. I'm really confused because I thought we were friends even without the sex stuff, and I don't know if I'm bi or straight or what. I just wish he would talk to me. Are all gay guys only in it for their dicks? Signed, Bi-Curious Friend."

Nate flopped over on his back.

"Hey Bi-Curious, That guy is a major asshole. Run. Right into the arms of a guy who can and wants to help you figure this out. No, not all gay guys are in it for their dicks, any more than all straight guys are, but sometimes we're more honest about it."

Kellan tipped his head to see Nate's expression in the light from the bathroom. There'd been a trace of a smile, but now Nate's eyes looked serious, staring back at him as Nate went on in the same tone.

"You say you were friends for a long time before the sex stuff. Maybe he's the one freaking out because you're the one who changed the rules. Maybe he doesn't like to think of himself as your test drive on a stick shift. But if he's not talking to you, I guess you'll never know. Good luck, Gray."

"*Run.* You say that a lot."

"A lot of people are in really shitty relationships with selfish assholes."

"And you don't think assholes can ever change?"

"People are who they are. Someone who fucks up is usually going to keep doing it. Cheaters cheat and liars lie."

Kellan rolled onto his side facing Nate. "That's your philosophy of life? For an advice columnist you're a big downer."

Nate shrugged. "Try seeing some of the mail I get. People suck. Sometimes they just want me to give them permission to be bigger assholes to the people they love."

"I know what Gray would say to that, 'Run.' But you know what? I think he's full of shit."

Nate rolled away again.

On his way into the offices of Brooks Blast Energy Drinks' CEO, Kellan stopped to say hi to Tina, his dad's secretary. She probably knew more about Brooks Blast and the Brooks family then any of them. She gave him a sweet smile. "He's waiting."

The man and the office seemed smaller than they had the last time Kellan had been summoned to stand in front of his father's desk.

Geoffrey looked up as if he was surprised to find Kellan standing there, like he hadn't sent Shep out to bring him in. He hoped Shep would also be bringing him back. Kellan was going to need a map to find buses back to Nate's apartment.

"Kellan. Take a seat."

"I'll stand, thanks."

"I wanted to have our meeting in person so that I could be sure I have your complete attention, but to help you focus, this..." his father slid a computer-printed check across his desk, "...is a cashier's check made out for five hundred thousand dollars. And here is your phone, the account reactivated."

Of all the things Kellan missed, money, cars, having underwear that didn't give him a wicked wedgie all day, he missed his phone the most. He'd spent the first week reaching for it constantly. It was insane that with all that money on the table, Kellan was thinking more about his phone. The fact that his father had put it there said he knew it too.

"And is this payment for my time taking the meeting?" Kellan reached for the check, but his father put his hand over it.

"Not quite. I must say I'm impressed."

Kellan couldn't help the burst of pride that heated his chest. He couldn't remember the last time his father had given him any kind of compliment.

"And what's so impressive?" Kellan folded his arms across his chest.

"That despite your previous habits of chasing everything in a skirt, the Gray boy managed to turn you queer in barely a month. I have to hand it to him."

"I thought you'd decided I was faking it for attention."

"Initially I did, yes. But other information has come to light."

Holy shit. Did his dad have the apartment bugged? How else could he know what had happened last night?

"At least you have the decency to feel ashamed of it."

"I'm not ashamed." Not of that. Not one minute of it.

"Then why are you blushing?" His dad's disgusted tone made the uncontrollable burn on Kellan's cheeks sound like Kellan was fucking some guy right in front of him.

"Why are you such a bigot?"

"Name-calling. The final refuge of the loser in an argument. I hardly think it makes me a bigot to want my son safe, free of an unhealthy lifestyle."

Kellan tried to explain that he knew enough to not take risks, but his father cut him off.

"Don't tell me about your practices; I don't want to hear it. I'm not only talking about disease. Do you know how many men have lost careers and families by giving in to this? This kind of lifestyle is never going to be accepted. Perhaps I drove you to this, but I'm willing to have you back home, provided you abandon this thing with Leonard's boy."

"His name is Nate." When Kellan swallowed, it felt like there was a gigantic sandbag in his throat. "And you're wrong." Damn, that came out too soft.

"What?"

"I said you're wrong." Kellan's voice was stronger now. "You and a bunch of old guys aren't going to get to decide what people are allowed to do. People don't think like that anymore."

"That's wishful thinking by homosexuals and some deluded liberals. I've spoken to senators and governors. I've had to hear their concerns about my inability to manage my own household, let alone my business. I'm not going to get into a debate with you. This is unacceptable."

"Wow. For a minute I almost thought this had something to do with me."

"It has everything to do with you." His father opened an envelope, spilling out full-page pictures of Kellan and Nate. Not last night, when they'd actually been doing something, but Kellan resting his hand on Nate's shoulder as Kellan swung off the scooter, a trip to the market, Kellan waving a zucchini suggestively at Nate, the next shot showing Nate punching Kellan's shoulder and grabbing the vegetable away, an afternoon too hot to wait in the apartment, Kellan sitting on the steps outside, Nate's guitar over his knees. Kellan knew exactly what had made him look up and smile like that, the gasping cough of the scooter coming around the corner on Boyer Street. Hell, Kellan was smiling in every shot.

Kellan pulled one of the pictures closer. They were in the laundromat, Nate folding jeans while Kellan was telling some story, hands making some kind of measurement in the air. Nate was watching him, a half smile curling his lips. But it wasn't what was in that smile that made Kellan want to hide this picture from his dad, from anyone who wanted to judge Nate for that look on his face. There was something softening Nate's eyes, something different from all the times Kellan had seen him this past month.

Kellan's chest got tight and hot and cold all at the same time, and he grabbed the picture off the table. He couldn't stop the smile from breaking on his face, so wide his jaw—even his ears—ached, the crush in his chest making him dizzy. Careful not to crease Nate's face, he folded the picture and stuck it in his pocket.

"Well?" Geoffrey asked.

"Pictures don't lie, Dad. I'm gay. I'm in love with another man." *Holy shit. And he's in love with me.*

His father picked up a brass paperweight and slammed it down on Kellan's phone.

Kellan jerked away, but there was no shrapnel. "Now who's losing the argument?"

"If you leave now, Kellan, it's not just the money. You'll really be on your own. No protection."

"That almost sounds like a threat."

"Of course it's not a threat. Do you think I want something to happen to you? After Keegan?"

"Well, either way, I guess you get your wish. It'll be like I was never born."

"You're a hell of a negotiator."

But there was a tremble in his father's voice Kellan wished

he couldn't hear. "I'm not negotiating anything."

"I'll put another zero on the check. Five million, Kellan. That'll go a hell of a long way. I'll set you up with a financial manager, and you won't ever have to ask me for money again."

It wasn't the money but the desperation in his father's voice that held him there when all he wanted to do was get back to Nate.

"Dad, look at this." Kellan held up the picture of him playing the guitar. "Look at me. Couldn't you just be happy because I'm happy?"

Geoffrey slapped the picture away in a flash of rage, and Kellan wondered if his father would hit him. "Fooling around with some boy is not going to make you happy."

"Wrong again, Dad. It already has."

Kellan knew where the BBEx offices in Dundalk were in relation to Nate's apartment, but he had no idea what buses to take to get there. He had a twenty in his pocket, but in a rainy rush hour, he couldn't spot a cab anywhere.

He'd started slogging his way west when a car pulled up on the curb, slow enough to spare him the gutter douche. When he recognized the black Town Car, hope loosened some of the knots in his stomach. Maybe his dad had finally listened. Maybe his dad actually cared if Kellan was happy, instead of under control.

But when Shep rolled down the tinted window, Kellan could see the rest of the car was empty. "Need a ride?"

"Did he send you?"

"No. He's working late. I've got maybe forty-five minutes, so if you're getting in…"

Kellan jumped into the passenger seat. "Thanks, Shep."

His father's driver nodded and pulled away, whipping through traffic toward Butcher's Hill.

When Shep pulled up on the corner near Nate's apartment, Kellan tried to hand him the twenty from his pocket.

"No, thanks. I think you need that more than I do. Tina said to tell you good luck."

Kellan climbed out and then leaned back in. "Thank her for me." His father's secretary had always been nice to him, despite the way Kellan used her like his own travel agent when he was too lazy to book his flights and hotels. "And thank you."

"He's not a monster, Kellan. He does worry about you."

Kellan shrugged. He wasn't even that pissed at his father anymore. All he wanted was to go see Nate, to find out if what he saw in that picture was true.

Shep tipped his hat and pulled away.

Chapter Sixteen

Nate had a definite plan about wallowing in sheets that still smelled like Kellan, so when Eli pressed the buzzer for Nate's apartment, he thought twice—and then three times—about letting him in, but Eli kept pressing the buzzer.

At last Nate tapped the intercom.

"I'm not letting you freak out over this alone."

"I'm fine. Go home." Nate switched off the intercom, and Eli pressed the buzzer again.

With a wind-tunnel-force sigh, Nate let him in.

He knew why Eli was here. After a few people in the *Charming Rag* office had politely inquired about the bug up Nate's ass, Eli had been dispatched to get the truth out of him. Eli had set up an ambush when Nate left his office to pee.

And Nate had never been good at lying.

The brush-off Nate had given him at the office didn't stop Eli from appearing in his doorway now. "Of course he's coming back," Eli said, dropping his soaking umbrella in the hall.

"No. He's not."

"He loves you, the poor deluded soul."

"Eli, it was only a scam."

"What was?"

"The whole star-crossed lovers thing. Kellan's dad did toss him out, but for fucking everything in a skirt, not for being gay. Kellan just wanted to embarrass his dad, so he pretended to come out. I'm sorry. I should have told you."

"Bullshit. I know you too well. You'd never have gone along with that."

"I did." And he told him about their parents, and the formula, and the promise of exposing the Brooks Company's so-called cleanup bid.

"But I saw you. You guys—I mean, he did come across a little weird at first, but I thought that was because he'd been so closeted, but Kellan's not straight. Fuck, Nate, he had his tongue in my mouth."

Nate shook his head. He didn't really need the reminder right then. It was going to be hard enough to see Kellan with his hands all over his next bimbo on the gossip sites.

Eli grabbed Nate's arm. "I've seen him look at you. And that sure as fuck told me I wouldn't be getting another chance with you."

"Yeah, well, he's one hell of an actor. He should have stayed on TV."

"Oh, honey." Eli pulled Nate into a hug.

Eli couldn't help spilling his emotions all over any more than Nate could help wanting to give the guy a shove out the door so he could brood about this on his own. He tried to extricate himself from the comforting hug that was only making him more uncomfortable, when he heard the sound of big feet on the wooden stairs.

Nate's chest was already tight when Eli squeezed harder, astonishing Nate by lifting his feet off the floor a half an inch. So what if Kellan was back. It didn't mean he was staying.

Nate hadn't bothered to lock the upstairs door after letting Eli in, so the door swung open under Kellan's hand.

"I told you he'd come back." Eli ran and gave Kellan the same big-squeeze treatment, though Kellan's feet stayed on the floor.

"Was there a question about that?" Kellan looked at Nate. "Was I supposed to find someplace else to stay?"

"You can cut that stuff out, Kellan. I told Eli it was all a fake."

Kellan kept looking at Nate, like there was something Nate was supposed to do. Nate dropped his gaze and went to the fridge. Eli had brought over an X-treme Cream and a Tangococo. For Kellan.

"Fake, huh?" Kellan said. "I didn't know a guy could fake orgasms."

Nate coughed. Half the mouthful of cream soda went into his lungs, half went up his nose, and almost all of it ended up on his arm as he spluttered and wiped his face.

"Okay, baby?" Kellan patted Nate's back, hand then grasping his shoulder in a tight pinch.

Nate turned and rubbed his face into Kellan's shirt.

"You getting cream on me another way is exactly how I remember it."

Eli laughed. "I remember you liked the tangerine-coconut, so I got you one."

"Oh yeah, just one of the many things I couldn't get back home."

Nate dug his chin into Kellan's shoulder to get him down the last few inches Nate needed to whisper in his ear. "What the fuck is going on?"

Kellan's hand slid down Nate's back and cupped his ass,

while using his other hand to reach into the fridge for the soda.

Nate jerked free.

Kellan uncapped the soda and leaned against the sink. "So I guess you guys want to know what happened?"

"Duh." Eli rolled his eyes.

Kellan milked every last bit of attention, pausing to drink from the bottle so that Nate had to watch the bob of his throat, the motion of his jaw, everything he couldn't have. Why hadn't he taken advantage of the opportunity last night and tasted that skin, felt it with his tongue?

"My dad was impressed."

"Really?" Eli was a perfect fawning audience.

"Well, not with me, with Nate. Sorry, man. He thinks you turned me gay."

"Didn't I?"

"I thought that wasn't possible, Mr. Advice Column guy."

"For fuck's sake, Nate..." there went Eli's eyes again, "...you know sexual orientation is set by the age of six by the latest and probably in utero."

"And is also influenced by environmental factors," Nate added.

"Oh, like I had an absent father and that made me girlie." Eli held up a limp-wristed hand. "That is so retro, it's like the fucking fifties."

"Do you guys want to hear the story or not?" Kellan thunked the bottle onto the counter.

"Sorry, Kellan," Eli said.

Kellan looked at Nate.

"I'm not stopping you." What the hell did Kellan want from him?

"So my dad says he's getting grief from all those homophobic politician buddies of his and puts this check on the desk and says it's mine if I come home and fly straight."

"Did you rip it up?" Eli was almost bouncing on his feet like he was watching a parade. "Wait, how much was it for?"

Kellan shrugged. "Half a mil."

Eli staggered and slapped a hand against the counter. "I feel faint."

Nate heard some buzzing in his own ears. Five hundred thousand dollars might not be a lot to the Brooks family, but it went to hell and back in Nate's world.

And Kellan hadn't said whether or not he took it.

"I didn't rip it up." Kellan grinned. "I told him no. That I was happy right where I was."

"Did it occur to you that you could have cashed the check and then told your father no?" Nate suggested.

"There's always strings with the old man's money."

"Breaking news: Nate Gray is a fucking asshole. The man gave up a-a-a—I can't even say it, I'll pass out—a half a million dollars for you." Eli stabbed Nate with a pointed finger.

"Well, I wouldn't exactly call that breaking news," Kellan said with a smile.

"Thanks." Nate glared. "So where does that leave you?"

Kellan folded his arms across his chest. "I was kind of hoping here."

"Nate, if you don't blow him right now, I will."

"Eli—" Nate ground his teeth together and grabbed the grinning Kellan to haul him into the bathroom.

"Oh yeah. Do it right," Eli called after them. "I want to hear him this time."

Nate shut the door then leaned his head against it.

"So I guess that means you're not going to blow me?" Kellan's voice was too close, but there was no room to get away from him.

"Be serious for a second. What happened?"

"I wasn't lying. He offered me money, said he didn't like the idea of me being gay—"

"So he believed you now?"

"He had pictures."

Nate hadn't stuttered a word since he had speech therapy in first grade. "Last n-n-n-night?"

"No. Just us hanging around." Kellan dropped the lid on the toilet seat and sat on it, then pulled Nate into an awkward sprawl on his lap. "Now that didn't go like I thought it would."

Nate's knee throbbed where it had banged off the bathtub. "Because I'm not a girl."

"Yeah, I know that." Kellan let him up. "It's kind of the point."

"Pictures?" Nate rubbed his knee. That was creepy enough to make his gut squirm. Geoffrey had them followed? He was nuts. And who was to say he wasn't still doing it?

"Can we forget about my dad for a second?"

"I'm still freaking out about the pictures. What kind of pictures?"

"Nate." Kellan took his hand.

Now there was more to be freaked out about. Why was Kellan holding his hand? It was something you did when you had to give bad news. "Was it a private investigator? Should we talk to the cops? Isn't that an invasion of privacy?"

"Nate," Kellan said louder.

If it was bad news, if the stuff about walking out on his dad was another game he'd been playing in front of Eli, Nate wasn't sure he wanted to hear it.

"I think I'll—"

Kellan grabbed Nate's head and kissed him. Big hands held his face still, thumbs pressing on his cheeks, right above the line where he shaved, but the mouth on his was soft, coaxing. Kellan might be holding him in place for it, but he didn't try to take charge of the kiss, almost as if he'd gotten this far and forgotten what to do.

Nate parted his lips and flicked his tongue, and Kellan's tongue followed him back, bringing with it the taste of his mouth, the rain, the soda and the memory of Kellan moving under him last night, the stroke of their cocks together. Blood pulsed and throbbed along Nate's dick now with just the sweet drag of Kellan's tongue against his.

Nate broke free. "What the fuck is that for?"

"Because I wanted it—you. And because you wouldn't shut up."

"I don't understand."

"I, I, I, me, me, me. Nate, I know it's hard, but tear yourself away from yourself for a second." But Kellan whispered the words into Nate's lips with a smile so it was hard to be pissed. "I told my father I was really gay. And in love with you. And he said that was it. Done. Over. He means it."

Nate wanted to ask what Kellan meant—if he meant—but that would be another me thing, so he didn't say anything.

"And you're just going to look at me?" Kellan said.

"You know you can stay here. I said two months, but if you need longer—"

"Motherfucking shit, what's it going to take?" Kellan

pushed Nate back against the door and got down on his knees. He put his hands on Nate's belt, unhooked it. "I was ready before and I'm ready to prove it now."

Kellan looked up at him, and Nate watched his hand cup the back of Kellan's head. He hadn't meant to do that, meant to grab his belt and put a stop to this, but Kellan was on the top button of his fly. "I want to be here, Nate. Whatever it costs. Whatever it takes."

Something had seriously gotten fucked in Nate's nervous system because he was dragging Kellan's face into the crotch of his still-zipped jeans, holding Kellan there to rub against the ache burning down to his thighs. Nate hadn't decided on any of that, and it was still happening.

Kellan groaned and wrapped his arms around Nate's thighs. Jesus, Nate could come like this, the damp heat of Kellan's breath, the vibration of his groans, a little friction when his chin dug in. Kellan wouldn't even have to—but he was pulling down the zipper, shoving jeans and briefs out of the way.

Nate tried to make himself say, *It's okay, you don't have to,* but Kellan looked up and stroked Nate's dick with a sure fist, and Nate couldn't. He tried to make a few bargains with himself: *It won't be as hard on him if he doesn't go down too far, if I don't come in his mouth, if I blow him afterward.*

Swiping his tongue across his palm, Kellan shifted hands and pulled Nate to his lips.

"I'm not going anywhere," Kellan murmured, and Nate realized his hand was still on the back of Kellan's neck.

Using a little pressure to tip Kellan's head up, Nate whispered, "Just the tip, Kell, it's all I'm going to need."

Kellan's lips parted in a smile, and then he wrapped them around the tip, licked across the slit and pulled off.

Nate could read the reaction to the bitterness on Kellan's face. "Yeah, it's kind of—"

"Shut up." Kellan licked him again, lapped all around the head, spit running out of his mouth.

"It's okay, baby. Right there, just suck it a little, I won't push."

Kellan muttered something that tingled against Nate's skin, but he sucked, tight pressure around the crown, and then used his hand on the shaft, bobbing, moving Nate's cock back and forth over his soft, wet lips and tongue.

Nate knew where he was, couldn't for a second forget what was happening, but he needed... He cupped the back of Kellan's head again, fingers threading through the thick hair. "Look up at me, baby, please."

Kellan did, and the sight of him there made Nate's knees buckle and his hips shake. Kellan tried to go farther down and coughed. Thank God he kept his teeth covered.

"Don't worry about, oh, Jesus—"

Kellan tried to slide down again.

"Here, baby, hold your head like this and relax." All those promises were flying out the window. God help him, he'd tried. "I won't choke you." Nate rubbed a hand across Kellan's cheek, along his jaw. "Like that, yeah." He slid in deeper, backing off fast, slow slide in and then out, never all the way, but all the good soft parts of Kellan's mouth were squeezing and rubbing on Nate's dick. "That's it." He moved faster.

Kellan's hand fell away, and Nate was using Kellan's mouth, but it was too damned good to stop.

"Pull off, baby, I'm gonna come."

Nate thought he might have heard "Fuck that" before the rush from his balls flooded him with pleasure, blotting out everything but the way his dick felt so perfect shooting in Kellan's mouth, shuddering every bit of sensation out of him until he sagged against the door. He slapped his hand out to hold himself up and snapped the bar off the towel rack.

Kellan sat back and wiped his mouth and chin on the back of his hand. "That's, um—"

"They say vegetarians have better tasting come." Nate couldn't believe that had jumped out of his mouth. In fact, he was a having a hard time believing almost anything he'd done since Kellan had knelt in front of him.

"So that's why you are?" Kellan rolled to his feet. "Does it get you more head?"

"Doesn't hurt to mention it."

Kellan leaned in and kissed him. It wasn't exactly a snowball, but there was plenty to taste. "So what do you think?"

"I think..." Nate's knees finally gave out, and he sank onto the floor, "...that I don't fucking know anything."

"That's what I've always wanted to hear you say."

Chapter Seventeen

Dumbfounded worry wasn't exactly what Kellan had been hoping to see in Nate's eyes, especially not after Nate had made those sounds as he pumped a bitter load into Kellan's mouth. About which, Kellan was brushing his teeth. Right now.

It wasn't until Kellan had gotten back to the apartment and Nate had started acting like seeing Kellan come back was somewhere down on his list of favorite things to do between cleaning the toilet and dying of malaria that Kellan realized he'd staked his life on a look in a photograph. He'd never actually seen Nate look at him like he had in the picture, and he sure as shit wasn't looking at Kellan like that now.

He scrubbed at his tongue. He'd really liked having Nate's dick in his mouth right up until he shot. Kellan was sure he'd get used to it. He hadn't really liked beer at first either, but the buzz was worth it.

He kind of thought Nate would leave the bathroom, but he dragged his ass up and started trying to fix the towel rack he'd knocked on the floor, glancing over at Kellan from time to time as if he was going to somehow evaporate. That was the only way to get out of the bathroom with Nate standing there in front of the door, unless Kellan tried to go through him.

A little touch would be nice, considering that the other effect those sounds had on Kellan was to make his rock-hard dick leak like a fucking faucet in his jeans.

A bang startled Kellan into spitting in the sink as Nate started wailing on the end of the rack with his palm to force the bar back in place. Like he was the one feeling a little frustrated.

Kellan rinsed out his mouth and wiped with his hand again. That still smelled like Nate—the smell way better than the taste—and it only made Kellan's dick harder.

"That bad, huh?" Nate nodded at the sink.

"I hear it's mostly sugar, and I can't afford a dentist."

"There is that."

Kellan had been counting on Nate actually knowing what he was doing with the whole gay thing. Nate had the sex part down okay, at least as far as bossing around the guy who was trying to get him off, but his after-sex moves needed serious work. Like now. Like what about some attention for Kellan's dick? Was he supposed to stick himself in a cold shower?

Nate put his hand on the doorknob. Out there was more room to execute a classic Gray-run, invent a need to leave or hide behind Eli's attention-grabbing drama. Kellan wasn't ready to give Nate up to that. Not at least until they'd settled a few things.

Kellan put his hand on the door. Nate looked up, the question in his clear brown eyes still not what Kellan was hoping to see.

For all Nate said he wasn't a chick, Kellan couldn't believe he had to do the asking. "So, two guys walk into a little room. Both their dicks get hard, but only one gets off."

The eyes Kellan was watching so closely widened in surprise, then Nate put his palm against Kellan's crotch and rubbed.

"That does seem to be a problem." Nate's fingers tightened

around the length and he stroked again. "But why is it a problem for the guy who got off?" he murmured.

"Because that guy could get a reputation as a cock tease. And then how would he ever get laid again?"

"That is a problem." Nate slid his hand down the waistband of Kellan's thankfully loose jeans, but they were only loose enough to let Nate's hand work in tiny jerks.

"You're the advice columnist." Kellan pushed the words out as his breath came faster.

"My solution to the problem is for the guy who got off to give the other guy the best handjob of his life, and the problem will be solved."

"A handjob, huh?"

Nate freed his hand and spun Kellan around so that his back was to him. With a nudge of his knee, Nate pushed Kellan to the edge of the tub and unfastened his jeans. "A handjob."

There was the thunk of an open cabinet behind them, then Nate was back, hand slick and warm as it stroked the shaft. The heat built until Kellan knew it was one of those special lubes that get hotter with friction. He wanted to accuse Nate of cheating, but damn, it felt nice.

"Because when I blow you, Kellan, you're going to be really glad it wasn't in this tiny little bathroom." Nate's fingers now slipped over Kellan's balls, tracing the shape like a couple warm wet tongues, then cupping him until the palm felt like a mouth, holding his whole sac while the same wet hot pressure worked his shaft as Nate used both hands on him.

"Why?" Kellan gasped the word out.

"Because you're going to need lots of room to spread out and go crazy."

"Yeah."

"Gonna be so good."

That kind of let's-wait bullshit wasn't much different from the excuses Kellan had given Delia the last month of their engagement. Was this why he couldn't go through with it? Because what he'd really wanted was another guy—Nate—to do this to him?

A twist to the strokes, thumb paying special attention to the spot right under the head. Oh hell yeah. There were definite advantages to having another guy jerk you off. Strong sure grip, broad solid body to lean back into while you concentrated on the feelings.

"I'm going to use my mouth on you like this. Then I'm going to finger your ass." As Nate went on in that hoarse whisper, his finger slipped under Kellan's balls, spreading heat and sensation along the skin there, skin so thin it seemed like Nate's finger was already in him.

"Fuck." Kellan's throat trapped the word so it came out high and tight.

"You can tell me that later. After I do it. You can tell me if you want it. And if I do it right, you're going to beg me."

A teasing, darting pressure that rearranged a lot of what Kellan thought he knew about his body, and then Nate's attention was all on Kellan's balls and dick, pushing him hard now, forcing him closer. Kellan reached back blindly, got a hand on Nate's head and another one on his hip and let Nate take more of his weight.

When Nate had gotten all pushy during the blowjob, Kellan's dick had liked it. Now Nate was claiming he'd make Kellan beg for something he wasn't sure he wanted.

Kellan's dick didn't have any doubts. That promise made all systems go for launch. "Harder. Right under the head. C'mon, man."

And Nate did. The best hand job of Kellan's life ended with him swearing that he shot sparks from his dick, or maybe the sparks were behind his eyes, because he shot ropes of come over his best friend's hand, flying out of him until he heard them splash into the tub. Pleasure echoed back after every spasm until everything tingled from his hair to his toes.

He was still gasping when Nate's grasp shifted to around Kellan's waist. "You good?"

That was a stupid question. "Fuck yeah."

Nate released him and handed him a towel, moving to the sink to wash his hands.

"That heated stuff going to give me a rash?" Kellan's dick felt raw, but not from the lube, from all that sensation. He had seriously been overlooking the potential of hand jobs. And if Nate was that good with just his hand...

"Not that I know of. It's not waterproof or anything."

By the time Kellan had finished cleaning himself up, Nate had his hand on the doorknob again. That was how this had all started, but no matter how much he might want to, his dick wasn't up for another round yet.

Nate was about to escape through that door, but Kellan was okay with that right now. Nate would have to get back into their bed again sometime, and now Kellan knew Nate couldn't turn down what Kellan was ready to offer.

As if he could feel Kellan's stare, Nate looked up, eyes still confused. "What?"

A confused Nate was better than a running-away Nate, so Kellan shrugged and said, "I didn't say anything," before dropping a quick kiss on Nate's lips and putting a hand over Nate's to turn the knob.

Kellan hadn't been sure if Eli was still going to be there and was really glad to find the apartment empty.

That didn't stop Nate from trying to put some distance between them. "Where did he go?"

Right now, Nate's tiny apartment was the perfect size. Nate had his choice of the bed or the kitchen. Kellan easily cornered him at the counter.

"I was busy sucking your dick, so I don't know."

Yin jumped up on the counter and started swatting around a piece of paper.

Nate reached for it, but Kellan beat him to it.

"There's no name on it," Kellan pointed out when Nate held out his hand. "But I'll read it for you. 'Sorry, guys. I got tired of sticking my fingers in my ears, and I figured Nate would queen out if I jerked off in the apartment. Unless you're sneaking Viagra, thought you might have to come up for air and might want to celebrate at The Arena. It's not raining now, but I could probably get Casey to give us a ride back over. You are totally my heroes. Text me. P.S. You really need to change the sheets.'" Kellan looked up. "Queen out?" He had never heard that before, but it kind of fit Nate when he got ranty. "I like that."

"Don't get attached."

"To the expression or—"

"You said before you wanted to go to a club." Although Nate met Kellan's gaze, the look still wasn't there. In fact, he looked more on the verge of a queen out, like something was ready to explode.

"If you want to go." Kellan kept his voice even, not wanting to get a face full of whatever Nate had bottled up.

"I should. He was trying to be supportive coming over here, and I think he's kind of counting on it." Nate slipped around the other end of the counter and grabbed a shirt from the dresser.

"Well, if Eli's counting on it, we should definitely go."

Nate spun back. "What does that mean?"

It means I should have kept my mouth shut. "Nothing."

"You're the one he has a crush on now." Nate yanked the clean shirt over his head.

Kellan had gotten the idea that Eli didn't exactly run a tight budget on his affections and couldn't figure out why Nate was acting jealous. "Why are you pissed off at me?"

"I'm not mad at you. I had a shitty day. Then all this happened and now I just want to go out."

"*All this* being I blew you?" How the hell did this get from maybe more sex and maybe a little I-love-you-Kellan to crap so fast?

"Did you want a *My First Blowjob* T-shirt?"

"Not exactly." Kellan wanted to put his hands on his head to try to squeeze out the headache anger had stirred up behind his eyes. Instead, he checked to see if his key was in his pocket and then headed out the door. "God, you're a bitch. See if I do it again."

Chapter Eighteen

"Wait. C'mon, Kellan."

Kellan was almost pissed enough about the T-shirt crack to ignore the sound of Nate running after him. He slowed down but didn't turn around. There'd better be an apology in there somewhere.

"C'mon," Nate said again.

Kellan kept walking.

"I shouldn't have taken my bad day out on you."

Kellan spun around. "Yeah. Your day must have really been tough compared to mine, right?"

Nate jogged and caught up with him as they hit the main street. "Okay. I didn't have a major scene with my dad, but I thought you were happy about that."

Kellan grunted a laugh. "I was."

"I don't know what you're expecting from me."

Kellan stopped walking. "Maybe you could think about someone not you for a second. Maybe you could stop pretending you don't want it before you shove your dick down my throat. Maybe you could help me while I'm trying to figure this shit out."

Nate stared at him. People with Friday night plans flowed around them with an occasional glare or a nudge, but Kellan ignored them, ignored the way his pulse was throbbing everywhere under his skin as he waited for Nate.

The stare turned into something else, not that look he'd been waiting for, damn it, but something that gave Kellan's circulation something to do besides carry around that useless adrenaline. A sexy blink, the slow curve on Nate's lips, a look that made Kellan think Nate had only been pretending to let Kellan get away before he pounced.

"You were pretty fucking amazing, if that helps."

Kellan swallowed. He'd never spent much time thinking about another guy's attractiveness, only judged them based on whether the girls the guy got could have done better. Nate was just...Nate. His best friend. But when Nate's eyes lit up like that, he wasn't just Nate anymore.

"Amazing?"

"Oh yeah. C'mon. I'll spring for a cab. Don't want you to get worn out."

There was a line outside the club. Sound poured through the cinderblocks hard enough to make puddles ripple. The entrance was down an alley that stretched along the warehouse-like building. There was enough of a breeze to chase off the heat from the day, but it wasn't cold. Still, lots of the guys in line were cuddling or hugging, so Kellan put his arms around Nate from behind, hands tucking into Nate's front pockets.

"What are you doing?"

"Being your boyfriend." Kellan kissed his ear. "You see, when one guy says fuck you to his homophobic father and a big pile of cash, then gives another guy a blowjob in the apartment that the other guy has invited him to share, they're boyfriends. Even a former straight guy can figure that out."

Nate turned around. "Wait. You really mean this? Not because of your dad or because you want to get off?"

"For a smart guy, you're an idiot, Gray. That's what I've been saying all night. What do you think I came back for?"

Nate's head tilted and his eyes—

The look broke something inside Kellan and made everything right at the same time. How could one look say so many goddamned things? And Kellan was so fucked because love was a hundred times worse than all the stupid songs could ever try to explain. And when he loved you back, it was too much. Like all of those feelings could never fit. You'd have to spend your life trying to figure out how, but it wouldn't matter as long as he kept looking at you like that.

Nate grabbed Kellan's head and kissed him.

Kellan wished their first real kiss could have been something special, something that didn't happen in an alley with a bunch of other guys standing around laughing and clapping.

"We're going back right now," Nate whispered in Kellan's ear.

"I thought Eli was counting on this."

"Fuck him. And I'm going to fuck you."

The idea rippled across Kellan's skin like a shock of electricity. He wrapped his arms around Nate tighter.

"Hey, faggots. Fucking cocksuckers." The taunt echoed down the alley.

Kellan looked up. There were only three punks and about fifteen guys waiting to get in. Why didn't someone say something?

"That's right." He turned to face the assholes who were screwing up the best night of his life. "Which would explain why you were sucking me off last night."

Amid the laughter and cheers, Kellan heard, "You're fucking dead, faggot."

Nate wasn't laughing as he pulled Kellan out of line. "What the hell are you doing?"

"Getting rid of those punks."

"You're not playing the ice-cream scene in *Witness*."

"Huh?"

"This is reality, not some gay Disneyworld you're vacationing in."

For someone who didn't have a TV, Nate was dishing out so much pop culture Kellan was getting ADD. Time to get the focus back on what mattered.

Kellan lowered his voice. "I'm not on a vacation, man. What part of your dick in my mouth isn't making this clear to you?"

"The part where this is just another role you're playing. Playboy Kellan, Reality-TV Kellan, Businessman-in-law-to-a-Senator Kellan and now what? Poor-Misunderstood-Gay Kellan, in love with the boy next door. Ding. Another month, time for the next costume change."

Nate stopped, or maybe he ran out of breath, but Kellan knew what was going on. It was a big fucking deal. And Kellan was scared too, but he wasn't letting either of them run this time.

"Stop hiding behind all that bullshit, Mr. Advice Column Gray. God, you're still the same terrified kid I had to teach to stand up for himself." Kellan leaned back against the building.

Nate had always been smaller, but the way he loomed in close, hands against the bricks on either side of Kellan's head, made Kellan want to straighten out of his slouch.

"I'm not the one who hid that year. I'm not the one who got

so scared by the idea of it he had to act like a homophobic jackass to prove himself to his friends."

"I should have known you wouldn't let that go so easily. Nathan Gray, always perfect, never makes a mistake. Until you started getting a little light in the loafers, my dad wanted me to be more like you."

The spark of anger faded from Nate's eyes. "Light in the loafers?" The corner of his mouth lifted.

"That's the way Geoffrey put it."

"Hey, you guys going to fuck out here or what?" The bouncer leaned over the edge of the stairs. The rest of the line was gone.

Nate turned away.

Kellan grabbed his wrist. "You get that I want to be here, right? That I want to be here with you."

Nate nodded. "But you've got to understand that you don't wake up one morning and decide—on the basis of one blowjob," he added as Kellan started to interrupt, "that now you're gay, end of story."

They dug out their IDs and Nate paid the cover.

Before they got so far in that the music thudded too loud to talk, Kellan leaned into Nate's neck. "If you think I woke up one morning with that idea, you haven't been paying attention."

The beat pounding up through the soles of Kellan's feet wasn't all that different from any other dance club he'd ever been in. He'd always thought of dance clubs as kaleidoscopes with people in them, spilling and regrouping in all different formations to the spin of the bright-colored lights. But inside The Arena, the energy wasn't fragmented like that. It was the same heat, same want, the same drive making the crowd on the dance floor move like one giant animal.

Eli bounced over to them before they had made it around the dance floor. Kellan suspected that Eli had already made more than a few trips to the bar area, since his usual enthusiasm was bordering on squirrel-on-crack behavior and his words were a little more lilty.

"Boys." Eli stretched up to give each of them a sloppy kiss. Though Kellan leaned in to meet him halfway, the kiss landed mostly on his chin. "Thank God. I was getting seriously bored."

"I find that hard to believe." Nate patted Eli's ass.

Kellan took another look around. There were a few guys dancing up on speakers, and they weren't wearing a whole lot.

"It's a sad, sad truth." Eli pouted. "I've had everyone in here worth doing. You excepted of course, gorgeous." Eli winked at Kellan. "So, can I borrow your boyfriend for a dance?" Eli looked at Nate, but he was already dragging Kellan away.

"Have fun." Nate waved.

Eli threaded his way through the shifting motion of the men dancing until he found a spot he liked, right in the middle, where the lights circled and flashed the brightest. Kellan didn't think he had great moves, but none of the girls he'd danced with had ever laughed. But none of the girls he'd ever danced with moved like Eli. The grace, the sway, the grind was sexy in a way Kellan had never thought about, and there was nothing feminine about any of it.

With the guys all shifting around him and Eli doing most of the dancing, Kellan just let the beat keep his feet and hips in motion.

"Thank you," Eli leaned in to yell.

"For what?"

"Now everyone's looking at me." Eli spun and shimmied his back down Kellan's front before turning and gripping Kellan's shoulders to pull him close and get their hips together.

"Eli."

Eli moved up and down so that when Kellan moved his hips to the beat, their crotches touched.

A flash of heat under his skin was the only warning before Kellan was hard. And shit, so was Eli.

"Eli, man, stop. Off." Kellan grabbed the guy's hips and held him away.

"Aw, what's a little frottage among friends?"

So that's what dry humping was called. Kellan filed that away.

"C'mon, dude. You're ripped." Kellan wrapped his arm around Eli's shoulders and pulled him out of the middle of the writhing crowd.

"I'm barely two sheets to the wind."

"Five at least." The area Kellan found on the second floor was dark and high traffic, but there was a spot with a counter full of abandoned drinks to prop Eli against and a chance to talk without screaming. "What's wrong?"

"Nothing. I'm happy for you guys, really."

Nate might think that Eli had switched his attention to Kellan, but it was obvious that Eli was still hung up on Nate.

"Ah. Sorry, man."

Eli shrugged. "I knew the first time I saw you with him, but today he was upset and he was so sure you weren't coming back. And Nate's always right, you know?"

Kellan did know. Or at least, Nate always had to be right and would make the facts fit whatever he'd decided was the truth.

Eli nodded as if he was hearing what Kellan was thinking.

"He's really a good guy, smart, and he cares about stuff, and damn he's a hell of a fuck—but I don't have to tell you that."

There was an idea. Eli was so shitfaced he probably wouldn't remember most of this conversation. And the fact was, Kellan hated flying blind.

"Actually, I could use a little telling."

Eli blinked up at him, eyeliner smudged with sweat. "What do you mean?"

"Well, you know how you said Nate's pretty vocal, like how did you mean? Like he moans a lot or he gets really bossy?"

"Well, I meant bossy, like the toppy, dirty talk but—wait, how come, are you saying you guys aren't having sex?"

"No." Because they were, and Kellan didn't want Eli getting his hopes up.

"So..." Eli's eyes got comically wide. "You've been topping him?" He giggled. "I can't believe Nate would bottom for anyone."

Top and *bottom* hadn't been a part of Kellan's vocabulary any more than *frottage* before tonight, but he was pretty sure he understood the definitions. And what it meant about Nate, the fucking control freak.

"No. Look, Eli, remember how Nate said he told you that me coming out wasn't real, that I was just trying to get back at my dad?"

"Yeah, but—"

"That was true. At first. I knew Nate was gay, and I didn't have a problem with it, and I knew it would make my dad shit a brick, but then I—well, it's different now. I don't know when, but it got real."

Eli put a hand on Kellan's cheek, face suddenly serious and intent. "Wow. What's that like? Figuring out you're—gay? Bi?"

Kellan shrugged off the exact definition, since he wasn't sure a nice rack wouldn't still raise a flagpole, but as far as he was concerned, Nate was all that mattered. "What was it like for you?"

"I didn't have to figure it out. I always knew. It was a surprise to me that other people were straight and had a problem with it."

Kellan thought about it. "It's like soda. Like you've always loved tangerine-coconut, and someone says try the black cherry and you think, that's okay for some people but not for me, but then you see the black cherry and suddenly it looks really good and you taste it and damn, it might actually be what you always wanted."

"That should have gone in the interview." Nate came up behind them.

Kellan turned, cheeks flushing. He hoped Nate hadn't heard the part about the top-bottom stuff.

"Cherry soda, huh?" Nate said.

"Yeah."

"Okay." Nate nodded, a smile breaking across his lips and the look in his eyes that said he got it, he believed it, and maybe all this bullshit about gay/not-gay was going to go away.

Kellan followed the urge in those eyes and leaned into Nate's kiss. Kellan was getting into it enough to forget about everything but how nice it was to be kissing Nate, when Eli gasped.

"Fuck me. You're a virgin."

"Excuse me?" Kellan turned back.

"Eli, shut up," Nate said through clenched teeth.

Eli turned Kellan back to face him. "Pay attention now, Kellan. This is advice from a total nellie bottom. The first time hurts like a bitch. You're going to think you sat on a fire hydrant. Well, okay, sometimes that happens more than the first time. But you have to remember, it's so worth it. Because once it's in and he knows what he's doing—and trust me, Nate knows what he's doing—it's really good."

Throughout Eli's advice Nate had been trying to find a way to get between them, but short of reaching through Kellan and clapping his hands over Eli's mouth, there wasn't anything Nate could do.

When Eli paused, Nate snapped, "Christ, Eli, we had sex once."

"Yeah, but you fucked me three times." Eli held up four fingers. "See, what you want to do, Kellan, is relax, which you think is kind of impossible at the time, but if you use your muscles to take him in, that makes it easier in the end." Eli's eyes widened and then he burst into laughter. "In the end."

"Jesus, I'm going to kill him."

"Nate, c'mon. He's..." Kellan leaned over, though whether he could manage to get loud enough for Nate to hear him without Eli hearing too was up for grabs. "He got drunk because he's upset about you."

"Me? That was four months ago."

"Never mind, Kellan." Eli put a hand on Kellan's arm. "He's a prick. In fact, I was only ever in love with his cock. Now, remember my advice and you boys have fun. I need to find someone else to fantasize about."

Kellan looked at Nate.

"I know. We can't leave him like this." Nate sighed. "You keep track of him, and I'll call a cab."

Chapter Nineteen

Nate was starting to think he'd need to run an account with the cab company. Before Kellan moved in, he'd call a cab maybe twice a year unless there was some kind of *Rag*-related emergency. His brain backed up along that train of thought. *Before Kellan moved in.*

Kellan had moved in, and according to Kellan, they were officially...dating? Boyfriends? Lovers? Nate wasn't going to dig at that. Because applying any kind of rational thought to the idea of Kellan having fallen in—infatuation, and deciding he was gay enough to have sex with Nate, ruined the incredible high of touching something that felt damned close to perfect.

Eli didn't give them much trouble or, as Nate remembered the look of panic in Kellan's eyes at the idea of getting fucked, any *more* trouble as they walked him out of the club. Nate had the idea that Eli wasn't quite as drunk as he was acting, that he liked being rescued, and despite his putting a few more hours between Nate and whatever parts of Kellan he was going to get at tonight, Nate didn't mind playing knight-errant.

If Kellan was even half right about Eli being hung up on Nate, he owed it to Eli for not having made it clear that a repeat—let alone a relationship—wasn't ever happening.

As they stepped out of the alley, Eli was taking advantage of his exaggeratedly compromised balance to cop a feel, using his arm around Nate's back to slide a hand over his chest and rub a nipple. Based on Kellan's lurch and cry of "Hey, now," Nate suspected Eli's other hand had wandered lower.

"I'm thinking three-way, right? It would probably be easier on Kellan if he had his dick in my ass the first time you fucked him. It'd be a hell of a way to get your cherry popped."

An electric shock of desire zapped Nate's balls. Brain on a conscience-free feed of Kellan caught between two male bodies, pleasure jolting through them as they all moved together. At the same time came an icy shower of jealousy, an irrational need to be the only one ever allowed to hear the sounds Kellan made while fucking, while being fucked. And if Kellan was going to fuck anyone...

"Thanks for the offer, man, but I'm sure Nate and I will work something out."

Between the HiDef stream of Kellan porn in his head and the distraction of dealing with Eli, the first thing Nate knew about the attack was a hard shove that sent him flying toward the street, face first into a parking sign. His cheek exploded with pain, at the same time he heard the sound of a fist hit flesh.

"Laugh now, faggots."

Nate straightened up. Just before his cheek went blissfully numb, he felt the wetness of blood, and then he grabbed at the guy who was punching Eli in the ribs. The same three punks from before. It had to be. Kellan shoved one of them off him, but an arm around Nate's neck yanked him from the man holding Eli. At least Eli had gotten free of them for a minute.

While he still had some breath, Nate yelled to Eli, "Run. Get help. Call 911." The last bit got choked off as the guy behind him tightened his grip.

"Fuck that." Eli slammed his head up into one asshole's

chin then kicked him in the balls. The guy dropped, and it was two on three. The guy on Nate's back got in a rabbit punch on his kidneys, and then Eli did a fancy kick thing to the guy's hip that loosened his chokehold, but he still dragged Nate on top of him as he fell.

Kellan punched the man in the face, and he finally released Nate. Kellan swung again to knock the guy flat, but the punk Kellan had been fighting managed to get in a good swing to Kellan's mouth. Nate was climbing to his feet to face another assault, but headlights flashed along the dead-end street, and the three bashers took off.

The cab pulled up close then started to drive away, but Kellan jumped in front of it.

Nate opened the door and they climbed in. Kellan was cradling his wrist in his lap and cursing.

Eli leaned toward the plastic partition. "Maryland General."

"No," Nate said.

"Yes. You need stitches and Kellan—"

"I think I fucking broke my hand."

"Thinks he broke his fucking hand," Eli finished.

"I don't need stitches." Nate put his hand up to his face. It throbbed now, an occasional sharp twinge when he moved his jaw, but when he looked down his hand was covered with blood.

"It's still bleeding and it's right under your eye," Eli explained.

Kellan was hunched against the door, muttering a constant stream of obscenities.

"When did you get so sober?" Nate asked.

"Right about the time the adrenaline kicked in. Thank God for those assholes in high school and getting someone to teach me how to fight."

Yeah, Nate had been the one who needed a physical rescue. Not much different from when he was in high school. He put take a self-defense course on his ever-lengthening list of resolutions.

The cops came while the doctor was stitching Nate's cheek. He'd been informed he was lucky the cheekbone hadn't broken when the metal edge of the signpost split it open.

Nate told the cops what had happened, but he couldn't give much of a description. White men around twenty, all with dark hair, one with a scruffy beard, all wearing black hooded sweatshirts. Nate hadn't been looking at their faces, but at Eli and Kellan.

Eli came in while the nurse ran through the wound-care instructions. "Kellan's back from X-ray. He was really going on about pain, so they gave him something to shut him up. Morphine, I think, in case they have to set it. His ring finger was dislocated."

Nate followed him into Kellan's curtained cubicle. He was grinning and staring at his hand, which looked more bloated than Elton John.

"Any more news?"

"Nope," Kellan said cheerfully.

"Oh yeah," Eli said. "Morphine. He was a big baby and the nurse felt sorry for him."

"It seriously fucking hurt, man." Kellan met Nate's eyes. "You look better. Still kind of like a Halloween mask, though."

Nate's hand went to his cheek, a solid block of ice from the lidocaine shot. "It's only eight stitches."

"Maybe you'll look like a pirate after."

"Fuck, he's stoned," Eli said unnecessarily.

The doctor came in. "There's a small bone chip from the dislocation, but no other damage. Probably only a bad sprain."

The doctor's accent had Nate placing him as from somewhere in the Balkans but couldn't guess on how to spell the name the doctor rattled off.

"What do you do for your work?"

"Um...help out at rehab places."

"So no fine motor coordination? Do you play an instrument? The piano?"

Kellan looked like he had to think about that.

"The guitar," Nate answered for him. "He works as an assistant to a recreational therapist. He plays the guitar as part of his job."

"Hmm," offered the doctor.

Kellan held up his hands like he was playing the air guitar. "Good thing it's not the fret hand."

"I will put a splint on the finger, but you must take these X-rays to an orthopedic doctor as soon as possible."

"Sure thing," Kellan said.

Nate wondered if Kellan wouldn't have given a thumbs-up to an amputation order while floating on morphine. He couldn't imagine what kind of scene Kellan had put up to get a shot. They hadn't offered Nate as much as a Tylenol.

The splint went on, though Kellan was disappointed that it wasn't, as he put it, his give-the-bird finger, and an aide came to tell them they were going nowhere until the social worker had been to see them.

"Right, no insurance. Jesus, we should have put your dad down as a responsible party. He probably wouldn't even notice the bill."

"Fuck him. I'll pay it."

"You've got three grand in the bank? And another couple for the ortho?" Nate asked.

Kellan blinked at him as if surprised by the news that medical care was neither cheap nor automatic.

The Medicaid paperwork took longer than the rest of the trip to the ER, but after Kellan had given his life history and awkwardly scrawled his name at the bottom of a promise to be financially responsible for the rest of the bill, they were finally free.

They took another cab and dropped Eli off first. He'd managed to escape with only a couple of bruises, including a darkening one on his jaw. A punch to his mouth wasn't enough to slow down its movement at all as he told them it was a good thing he hadn't been hurt since his insurance with the paper still didn't kick in for another month. Like Nate could fix that. He wasn't the owner.

Getting Kellan up the stairs wasn't too hard, though Nate doubted Kellan would remember anything about the trip. Nate dumped him on the still-unmade bed where he landed with an ominous clank of the metal supports.

Kellan lay there laughing for a few minutes and then propped himself up on his elbows, muttered an "Ow" and then flopped back again. "Aren't you going to undress me?"

"You can do that yourself."

Kellan held up his splinted hand. "At least get my sneakers."

With a sigh, Nate bent down and untied the laces then pulled off the shoes.

"And this button." Kellan gestured at his fly.

Nate looked at Kellan's face as he reached out to unbutton Kellan's jeans. "What is this, an interactive strip tease?"

Kellan laughed and thrust his hips up. "The zipper?"

"You're pushing it, Brooks." Nate pulled the zipper down, but before he could draw back, Kellan's good hand shot out and caught Nate's wrist.

"Yeah. Right where I want you."

"Kellan, I don't know if now—"

"It's okay. I know." Kellan dragged Nate's hand until it covered the bulge under the cotton.

Nate's fingers curved around the heat and the length, before sliding under the waistband to get his palm on the skin. Oh God, Kellan's skin. His cock. Nate licked his lips.

"Fuck me. C'mon, Nate, do it now. I'm feeling no pain."

Goddamn Eli.

"No."

With his good hand, Kellan pulled Nate on top of him. "Yes. C'mon, man. You owe it to me. I can't jerk off with this thing on, and I got it saving your ass."

"Eli might have saved my ass too." *Which doesn't stop me wanting to kick his for putting the fear of anal sex into you.*

Kellan reached up and cupped Nate's face. "I should have been there all those other times too. In high school. I'm sorry about that. I was freaked out."

"It's okay."

Hearing Kellan's stoned confession made Nate's stomach squirm with embarrassment. He didn't want Kellan saying—or doing—anything he wouldn't do sober.

"No it wasn't. You were the best friend—the only real friend I ever had."

"Okay. Why don't you try to sleep now?"

"You didn't take off my pants."

173

"Fine." Nate pushed to his feet and tugged Kellan's pants off his legs. "Need to pee?"

"Nope." Kellan reached for Nate again.

He let himself be dragged down against Kellan's chest, but when Kellan started grinding up into Nate's crotch, he rolled off to the side. "No sex."

"Why not? Please." Kellan gazed up with soft, pleading eyes. "I want you to fuck me. Want you in me."

Nate could see how Kellan had managed to get a dose of a level-one controlled substance out of the ER staff, but Nate drew the line at fucking someone who was in no condition to give consent.

"Kellan, you're too high to think straight."

Kellan laughed. "Don't want to think straight. I want a guy to fuck me in the ass. That's not very straight."

"It's not going to hurt that much."

"How do you know?"

"Because I've had bigger things than my dick in my ass."

"You can fuck your own ass?"

"No. I mean if you take your time, it won't hurt."

"Yeah, like you'd ever do it, ya control freak. Eli told me you don't bottom."

It sounded so strange coming from Kellan. He should be talking about some girl's boobs or a basketball score, not discussing sexual roles.

"I have."

"Tell me about it."

"Go to sleep."

"No. If you won't gimme sex, you have to at least talk to me about it." Kellan hooked one of his legs over Nate's.

"My first boyfriend in college always topped."

"What was his name?"

"Malcolm."

"Like the X guy? Was he black?"

"Yeah."

"What happened?"

"I figured out how much of a control freak I was."

"And now you always top."

"Pretty much."

"Pretty much?" Kellan lifted his head. "So does that mean if you won't fuck me because I'm high, I could fuck you because you're not?"

"No."

"Damn." Kellan dropped his head back against the mattress.

"Here." Nate grabbed a pillow and gently lifted Kellan's arm. "You're supposed to keep that elevated."

"I'm kind of nervous about it."

Nate decided to ignore what he knew Kellan meant. "Your hand will be fine."

"No, I mean about you fucking me."

But they were going there anyway. "Oh, baby, I'm going to make you love it."

"So do it now."

"If you still want to in the morning, I'll fuck you until you find a new religion."

"You're kind of different when you're talking about sex. You really let loose."

Sex had always been the one thing Nate could be sure of.

He wanted it, the other guy wanted it. From the first guy he'd blown sneaking around in high school, to Malcolm showing Nate about everything his body could do, right on up to now, sex was the one thing Nate never questioned. Until Kellan came along, there was no right or wrong about it, no wondering about why or what it meant. Now his only sure ground was quicksand. Kellan begging to get fucked, Kellan claiming Nate was what he wanted when Kellan had been the one to shove Nate away with both hands.

"You never talk dirty?"

"Not really." Kellan grinned. "But I like it when you do it."

Maybe there was an easy answer to this. Nate swung a leg over Kellan's hips and looked down at him. "You like me telling you what to do?"

Kellan nodded, Adam's apple bobbing while his hips bucked up against Nate's ass.

"So if I do something you don't want, you'll tell me?"

"Duh. So does this mean you'll fuck me now? I keep thinking about it, and I kind of want to get it over with."

"Get it over with?"

"You know what I mean."

"It's not an initiation. It won't make you any more gay, you know."

Kellan sighed so hard it blew through Nate's hair. "Why is that still even a question?" He sighed again, eyes blinking like he was on the edge of sleep. "I walked away from five million dollars for you."

"Five hundred thousand."

Kellan shook his head, lashes fluttering. "Five mil. Dad upped it when I wouldn't give in. So you'd better be worth it." Another sigh and Kellan was asleep.

Chapter Twenty

Kellan slept through the night and into the morning. Quan Yin curled into a ball next to him, her head on his uninjured arm, and snored softly. A few thicker gasps from Kellan had her shifting, but altogether, their little chorus made Nate smile as he made himself breakfast.

Nate found a contact number for the recreational therapist and called to let him know Kellan would be unable to play for awhile. The guy, Jeff, sounded more concerned about Kellan's injury than whether he would be coming to work, which only showed that Kellan's charm was universal. Jeff told Nate to tell his boyfriend—his boyfriend—that even if he couldn't play the guitar, they'd be happy to have him come in and help out with the clients.

Nate came out of the shower and looked at the boyfriend asleep in his bed, the one who expected Nate to be worth five million, expected Nate could provide all the answers when Nate couldn't explain it to himself.

There were things he could do to help Kellan start life as an adult at twenty-eight, but although columnist Nate Gray was full of advice for perfect strangers, when it came to understanding why Kellan thought Nate was what he wanted after all these years, he was stumped.

He worked on what he was good at, checking in with his

writers at the paper, sorting out assignments and proofing an article a freelancer had turned in. He told a guy who suspected his boyfriend was cheating on him to confront the cheater, and wrote a "Shades of Gray" rant about the fact that summer seemed like the time when it became convenient not to care about the homeless or the hungry because they no longer resembled something from a Dickens book shivering in the street.

Nate was sitting back down at his desk with a fresh cup of green tea when Kellan started to shift around on the bed. Yin jumped off and headed for her perch on the kitchen window. Nate leaned back in his chair and watched Kellan drag himself awake. A quick wince as he tried to use both hands to push himself up, and then he rolled to face Nate.

"Hey." Kellan's husky voice gave Nate a low-down tingle.

"Hey." Nate sipped his tea.

"It's morning."

Nate looked at his phone. "Afternoon, actually."

"Still."

Nate knew what Kellan meant. "How are you feeling?"

"Hungry and thirsty. My mouth feels like something furry died in there last week." Kellan rubbed his mouth and grinned. "Oh, and horny."

"A dead furry mouth is kind of a mood killer."

"So I'll get on that."

"How's your hand?"

"Hurts. Finger's better."

Kellan inhaled two slices of cold pizza and two glasses of water before heading into the bathroom.

There were a million reasons why Nate knew this was a bad idea. He'd never been with someone who'd never been fucked
178

before, he still didn't know that Kellan wasn't doing this because he thought he had to prove himself, and hell, as good as Nate knew he was in bed, no one was worth five million dollars.

But Kellan came out of the bathroom in nothing but a little steam and the drops of water running from his hair, and headed right for Nate. No matter how loud that negative voice in his head was, Nate knew that this was ending with his dick in his best friend's ass.

Kellan looked at him and shut that voice up mid-warning. "Stop stalling and fuck me, Gray."

Nate pushed up from the chair and pulled his shirt over his head.

"No music?" Kellan grinned as he knelt on the bed.

"What do you want to get fucked to?"

"Anything that doesn't sound like our having sex is some obligation that you've got to get through."

"I don't feel obligated." Nate found a site that streamed slow jams and turned the speakers up before peeling off his jeans. "Not even five million dollars worth."

"You still can't lie for shit. I shouldn't have told you that."

"You remember that?"

"Every word." Kellan waited in the middle of the bed. "I'm ready to find my new religion." He dropped onto all fours— threes, since he was still favoring his right hand—and waggled his ass in the air.

Nate lowered himself on top of all that skin that was cool and damp from the shower and felt Kellan shiver under him. "You're not ready. But you're going to be." He shoved Kellan's shoulder to turn him onto his back.

He kissed him, nothing soft or coaxing about it, kissed him

until both Kellan's teasing and that warning voice were distant memories. Kissed away all the weirdness of planning it, of being in bed with his best friend. Kissed him until there was nothing but the heat of tongues and cocks sliding together.

Reaching for Kellan's dick, Nate stroked him full and hot and hard before rolling the heavy sac beneath under his fingers.

"Yeah, do it now." Kellan's voice was straining behind clenched teeth.

"I should. Give you the fucking pounding you've been begging for. You deserve it the way you've been cockteasing me crazy for weeks."

Kellan's eyes widened.

"All those nights of you rubbing on me, the way you stare at my dick, my mouth. The way you just dropped to your knees yesterday." Nate fumbled behind him into the drawer of the end table.

"So what kept you?" Kellan wrapped his legs around Nate's hips and dragged him back down.

"I wasn't ready," Nate admitted. "But I am going to tease the ever-loving fuck out of you."

"No." It was a definite whine. "C'mon. I feel like I've been hard for a fucking month already. Please."

"It's been two minutes."

"I don't care." Kellan's voice edged deeper. "Shit, it's all I can think about."

Nate rocked against him while Kellan kissed and nipped at Nate's jaw and throat, tongue flicking behind Nate's ear.

"Do it," Kellan whispered again.

"Gotta let me up, baby."

Kellan lowered his legs, and Nate slid between them, tongue lapping along the trail of hair before he closed his mouth over Kellan's dick. A wave of heat washed through Nate, and he forced himself to remember this wasn't about what he wanted, though the sound Kellan made was so sweet, his cock filled Nate's mouth so right, he could stay here forever.

Kellan sighed, hand slipping through Nate's hair. Nate wanted to make this the best sex of Kellan's life. Not because Nate was a control-freak perfectionist, but for Kellan. Making Kellan happy could easily become the new number-one obligation in his life.

Nate mouthed along the side of the shaft and felt the skin tighten even more against his lips as the blood pulsed in the thick vein under his tongue. He licked Kellan's balls, then the thin smooth skin below, and Kellan's legs shook. Nate worked his shoulders beneath Kellan's thighs, forcing them farther apart, and flicked his tongue over the tight hole.

"Shit." Kellan jumped, but Nate's shoulders wouldn't let him move.

Nate licked again, reaching under Kellan's ass to lift him higher, dragging the flat of his tongue across the skin, using the point right at the entrance to make Kellan squirm and pant.

When Kellan finally relaxed and started trying to stay with Nate's tongue, he lifted his head to work his chin on Kellan's balls, rubbing against the sac while licking the base of Kellan's shaft.

Nate slid his hand around to find the lube he'd tossed on the bed and slicked up one finger. He tongued Kellan's balls harder, tracing the shape of what was inside, sucking one into his mouth while his finger circled and pressed. Kellan pushed down and Nate's finger slipped inside a tight heat that made his dick so hard he saw purple spots behind his eyes.

Kellan grunted and panted, and Nate didn't move the finger inside, but kept rubbing his thumb on the smooth perineum.

181

The muscles of Kellan's thighs were rigid, his breath fast and tight until Nate wrapped his lips around the head of Kellan's dick and angled his finger up.

He found what he was looking for in a salty spurt of precome in his mouth and a breathless groan in Kellan's chest. It was that purr again, deep and steady behind sealed lips, and Nate took Kellan's dick deeper into his throat as he started to fuck him with his finger.

For someone who'd never been anyone's first fuck before, Nate thought he was doing a damned good job until he went for two fingers and Kellan jerked away with a "Holy shit."

Kellan tried to remember Eli's advice about relaxing, but he was thinking more of the whole fire-hydrant thing he'd said. Since Nate's head was still down there, Kellan knew it wasn't a dick in him, but though Nate had stopped moving, Kellan's ass burned.

"What's in me?" Kellan looked down.

Nate kissed the head of Kellan's dick before saying, "Two fingers."

Two fingers? Damn. "Can we...?" Kellan wasn't sure what he wanted to happen.

"Want me to take 'em out?"

But Nate's motion had Kellan yelping, "No."

God, everything up to now had felt so fucking good. Nate's finger pushing inside in a way that felt sweet and hot everywhere, Nate's fucking tongue proving that Kellan's dick and balls weren't the only thing interested in oral sex.

"I told you I wanted to do this on the morphine."

"You are such a baby." Nate smiled. "Shut up and get over it."

Nate licked the head of Kellan's dick and twisted those fingers until they hit that spot again. Nate wasn't quite fucking him, just jabbing his fingers against that spot in the same rhythm as the bob of his head until Kellan couldn't remember why he'd had a problem with any of it.

He braced his feet against the mattress and drove himself down onto Nate's hand and up into his mouth, a steady stream of *oh fuck yeah* spilling from his lips. He was racing toward the edge, and he still hadn't gotten Nate's dick in him yet.

"Stop, I'm gonna come."

Leave it to Nate to go and fucking listen for a change.

But he didn't flip Kellan over and shove his cock in him, only eased out his fingers and stopped the hot pressure from his mouth.

The thing that pressed against Kellan's ass now was cold and hard and a lot smoother than Nate's fingers. As Kellan felt it start to slide in he knew what it was. That dildo. It didn't burn like Nate's fingers had, but the pressure wasn't exactly comfortable. The fake dick slid in farther and it didn't hurt, but God, it was too much, turning him into a giant raw nerve. Kellan didn't think it could get more intense and then Nate was sucking him again, and the dildo hit that spot inside.

Kellan's fists hit the mattress. "Nate." The name burst out of him, a warning and a plea.

Heat everywhere, the friction and pressure in his ass filling him up until it had to get free.

Nate's mouth rode him all the way through that explosion, and when he was empty and shoving Nate away, the sight of his come on Nate's chin triggered another round of shocks to recoil up his spine.

"God. That's fucking—holy shit. You can totally do whatever you want to me now." Kellan spread out across the

183

mattress, his bones turned to syrup from the pleasure still bouncing off his nerves.

Nate stretched out on his side, smiling down at him. "Better than morphine?"

"Better than my first blowjob. Totally." The pit of his stomach tingled in a nervous way, but he said, "I can take your dick now, no problem."

"Not yet."

"Why not?"

"Because I'm not fucking you until you're hard again. The next time you come, my dick's going to be up your ass."

The nervous tingle was now a big pit of want and fear. The dildo was nowhere near as thick as Nate's cock, and Kellan was sure Nate wouldn't be blowing him at the same time. But damn, that had felt good.

Nate rolled onto his back, and Kellan stared at his body. There was no doubt about it. The spot under the navel, the silky-looking hair dragging his eyes down, had become as interesting as the tease of cleavage from a low-cut blouse. No tease here, nothing cut off his view of Nate's dick, nothing left to the imagination—except exactly how that was going to feel inside him.

Kellan let his gaze roll the rest of the way down. Heavy hairy thighs had him thinking about how hard Nate could ride him, what it would be like to have him turn that power loose. A glance back up at Nate's face showed Kellan what he needed to see, Nate's eyes gone soft and open, crinkled with his smile.

"How're you doing?" Nate asked.

"I'm really, really good."

"Good. Is there any pizza left?"

Kellan threw a pillow at him and sat up. "I'll get the pizza, but if you drink any of that green-tea shit, I'm not kissing you."

"Nothing about my tongue in your ass, but the green tea is a problem?"

Kellan thought about it for a second and then leaned over and kissed him. Nate tasted mostly like come, and as Kellan sank back with him onto the bed, he realized that the smell they made together was turning him on.

Nate rolled him underneath. "No pizza?"

"No pizza."

Nate looked down, eyes happier than anytime Kellan had ever seen him. He reached up and ran his palm over the scruff on Nate's jaw before tugging him down for a longer kiss.

Things went slowly this time. Nate went slowly. He teased and licked and rubbed, and each time Kellan managed to get his eyelids to stay up Nate was staring down, the look in his eyes full of amazement, like he'd never had a guy in his bed before.

"What?" Kellan had to ask when he saw it again.

Nate's thick lashes dropped to hide his expression. "Nothing." But his voice was almost a whisper. And after he kissed Kellan out of his mind again, that look of awe was back.

His body felt good down to his toes from all that attention, but Kellan was still soft when Nate took him into a hot wet mouth. His erection built slowly, spreading out in fiery circles from his hips and down his cock, electric pulses fluttering from his balls and even that spot inside his ass. He squeezed those inside muscles, wanting something in there to keep that pressure building.

The back of Nate's throat rubbed velvet-slick and hot-tight on the head of Kellan's dick, buzzing him there as Nate groaned and took him long and deep and fast.

"Fuck me. God. C'mon, Nate. Get in there. I want to feel it."

Nate kept sucking while his fingers worked their way inside. It burned again, but Kellan didn't care because he knew how good it was going to get.

A twist from Nate's wrist and the stretch was hard enough to sting, but just as fast, Nate was pulling his fingers out.

Nate's hands got busy between Kellan's legs, and then he felt the brush of slick and cool latex against his thigh before it heated from Nate's dick.

"You're ready now, baby. You gonna let me in?" Nate breathed the words onto Kellan's lips and followed them with a deep kiss, tongue stroking inside.

"Want me to roll over?"

"No, like this. So I can watch you and kiss you."

With his arms under Kellan's knees, Nate lifted Kellan's legs almost to his shoulders while Kellan tried to make his body open up. There was something inside that needed this, more than just the way it felt good when Nate hit that spot in his ass, something that needed Nate touching him this way, looking at him like Kellan had something special only he could give him. He was wondering how many other guys had seen that look in Nate's eyes when Nate started to push inside.

Holy shit, the real thing was a lot bigger than the plastic dick. The pressure eased and came back, and Kellan really wanted to skip this part. Fast forward to the good friction and the coming and skip having to wrap his brain around the fact that something really big was making him feel easy to hurt.

Nate pushed again, and there was definitely a dick in Kellan's ass right now, and he wasn't sure this had been a good idea. Nate kissed him and groaned, not bossy or dirty-talking now, only whispering things like *good* and *yes* and *please, baby.*

Nate shoved Kellan's legs up farther, and Nate's balls rocked against Kellan's ass. Every single cell in Kellan's body felt fucked, full, owned.

"That's right, let me in all the way, Kell."

Kellan lifted his legs higher, rested his heels on Nate's back and dragged his head down for a kiss.

"Oh, yeah, you feel good."

Kellan wouldn't go that far, but it didn't hurt, and being this close to Nate felt right.

Nate shifted and moved goddamned deeper, little movements, like he was trying to get Kellan's muscles to stretch. He pulled out and then pushed back in, and the want-fear-need emptiness got bigger inside. So maybe gay guys were tougher than he was. Kellan was ready to give up on this gay sex thing, at least as far as ass-fucking went. Nate liked to fuck, and Kellan couldn't seem to get the hang of being fucked. Maybe Nate would be happy with just blowjobs. Then Nate pulled all the way out and slammed back in.

Kellan grabbed Nate's shoulders.

Nate looked down at him, and Kellan could put up with a lot more than a fat dick in his ass to get that look if it was all for him, clear brown eyes steady on his, smiling like Kellan was the best thing that had ever happened to him.

"Tell me you want it."

"Yeah."

"Say it, Kellan."

"Fuck me."

Nate grabbed Kellan's hips and started long slow strokes that hit deep in Kellan's guts, finding their way to that need until suddenly Kellan got why people did this.

"Fuck me, Nate. Feel so good in me. C'mon. Harder." Not

187

only because it felt good to have a cock working him there—
which it did now, Nate's cock rubbed that sweet spot with every
thrust of his dick. But it felt good in Kellan's chest too, filled in
something that had been missing. Kellan knew Nate never
looked at anyone else that way.

Nate kissed him, strokes shorter but harder friction, the
pressure inside pumping out through Kellan's cock.

Nate held him, stopped moving, and they both caught their
breaths.

"Holy shit, why weren't you ready for this the minute I
moved in?" Kellan could hear the echo of his voice in the rush
of blood in his ears, his fingertips, his dick and his ass.

"Because..."

"Don't lie."

"Things changed." Nate slammed his dick in hard.

"What. Changed?" Kellan gasped the words out, but he
wasn't ready to give in.

Nate's forehead pressed against Kellan's. "You know what."
His thrusts were slow and steady, belly in close to rub on the
crown of Kellan's dick.

Kellan threw his head back, and Nate dropped kisses all
over the stretched skin. "Tell me."

"After."

Kellan nodded. Nate was right. An *I love you* on the way to
orgasm wasn't something to put a lot of faith in, but Kellan still
wanted it. Wanted to know that he wasn't the only one who'd
never felt closer to anyone in his life, that the stupid promise of
smearing their cuts to make them blood brothers was nothing
compared to sharing their bodies like this, to knowing that the
person you wanted to share everything could share this with
you too, this amazing feeling of having someone inside you.

Nate kissed him, hands stroking everywhere, Kellan's hair, his face, his back as the pressure inside his body wound him up tighter.

"Jerk yourself off, baby."

Nate lifted up enough to let Kellan slide his left hand between them, and it didn't matter if he could barely make it work at this angle, the first two tugs on the too-tight skin were enough to get his balls climbing, temperature inside like a furnace.

Nate held his hips and thrust faster, their bodies coming together with a heavy slap of skin, barely audible over Nate's grunts.

"I'm—"

But Nate was already nodding like he knew, like there was a way to tell that Kellan was coming with his best friend's dick in his ass, and his entire soul was wrapped up in that explosion of pleasure.

"Oh Jesus, Kell. So fucking sweet." Nate's weight lifted and his fingers dug deep into Kellan's thighs. Nate moved fast, friction overwhelming, but when Kellan opened his eyes, the sight of Nate losing it, body shaking and mouth slack, was worth the burn. If Nate had been a girl, Kellan would have proposed the second Nate made that final deep slam inside.

For now, Kellan only watched Nate as his always-rigid pose melted, spine curling in, shudders hitting him from shoulders to hips, body jerking helplessly, and that was the most beautiful thing Kellan had ever seen.

They breathed and watched each other for a minute, then Nate leaned down for a sloppy kiss. "Okay, Kell, it's going to be uncomfortable when I pull out. Take a deep breath and let it out."

Uncomfortable   must   have   been   some   kind   of understatement for fuck-that-hurts-hurry-up, but then Nate was kissing all over Kellan's face, their sweat rolling together.

"You were so good. Fucking amazing," Nate breathed against his skin. "God."

Kellan stretched, enjoying every aching twinge in his muscles, even the funny not-quite soreness in his ass. "Yeah, I think that might have been worth at least four and a half million. But you still owe me five hundred grand."

"Later." Nate rolled in close, tangling one of his legs with Kellan's.

"That reminds me. Tell me that thing you were going to say later." Now would be a great time to hear that I love you, with his body still feeling sweet, Nate's fingers and breath teasing Kellan's hair.

"What?"

Nate couldn't have forgotten.

"About what changed."

"Yeah." Nate shifted his weight off Kellan. "You had to know I wanted to do that from the first time I saw you again."

"And?" Kellan prompted. It didn't sound like they were getting close to that I love you he'd been thinking about.

"But what changed is you wanted it too."

Chapter Twenty-One

Nate hadn't expected Kellan to discover a sudden passion for silence post-fuck, but with the narrowing of Kellan's green eyes, Nate wished the conversation had stayed on how awesome the sex had been. He leaned in to taste the sweat on Kellan's neck. What had he done wrong?

Kellan's jaw tightened. "That's all you were going to say?"

Nate pushed Kellan's hair off his sweaty face. "I thought it was kind of a big deal. Considering how you felt before."

"So you're saying it was just sex?"

"No. Definitely not that." Nate's hand slid along Kellan's jaw. "It was about us. But neither of us was ready for this when you came to stay last month."

That didn't do much to mollify the sullen look on Kellan's face, so Nate tried to kiss him out of it again, playing with his hair, breathing in the scent of their bodies together, the whole apartment full of the smell of their fuck. A little groan slipped out of his throat, and he cradled Kellan's head, fingertips rubbing the tight spot behind his ears.

Since he would have gotten more response from kissing the pillow, Nate raised his head.

Kellan wormed out from underneath.

"Is your hand bothering you? I've got Tylenol."

Kellan brushed a gentle finger at the cut under Nate's eye. He barely felt any pain now as worry started to seep into his muscles, turning all the good relaxation into nervous tension. Nate had definitely screwed something up.

"What's going on?"

"I need to tell you something. About when I was such an asshole to you back in school."

"Kellan, I'm over it. Really." Nate couldn't seem to keep his hands out of Kellan's hair, couldn't stop kissing the uncharacteristically thin line of his lips.

Kellan didn't pull away this time. "You don't get over anything." His laugh was dry. "But I still need to tell you this."

"Okay." The shimmery future Nate had managed to dream up in the past few seconds, a future where Kellan's big laugh and smile filled a bigger apartment, where their bodies tangled in a bigger bed every night, popped like the fragile bubble it was.

But maybe it was still fixable. Maybe there was something Nate could do, offer to show Kellan how it could be.

"Don't look like that. You didn't do anything." Kellan's lips curved a little.

"You're killing me here."

"After you told me you thought you were gay—"

"You didn't let me get it out."

"I left for camp the next week, remember?"

"Yeah." Summers were always so long until Kellan got back from camp that first week of August. Nate had kept a running tally of days in his head.

"I missed you a lot. I hadn't wanted to hear that, and then it—you—it was all I could think about. I was wondering if you were, then maybe I was."

Nate wished he knew what to say, what Hey Gray would say to Kellan if he'd written a letter.

"Why didn't you write or something?"

"I couldn't say it in my head. I wasn't going to put it on a piece of paper. There was another kid in my cabin—"

"Oh. That's nothing. Lots of kids try it out. It's not a big deal." A completely irrational disappointment burned in Nate's throat, but he covered it with a smile. "It doesn't matter if I'm not your first boyfriend." He reminded the hot spark of jealousy that virginity was a patriarchal construct, intended to insure primogeniture and keep women bound in fear with sexual inexperience. And when the hell did he get so fucking possessive? He kissed Kellan's forehead.

"Do you think you could shut up until I finish this?"

Nate had never heard that cold emptiness in Kellan's voice before. "All right."

"So this other kid—David—and me, we kind of had a feeling, and we started jerking each other off and stuff like that, hiding in the bathrooms or when we could get someplace alone."

Nate wanted to spill out more reassurance, whatever would chase that distant look from Kellan's face, but kept his mouth shut.

"We didn't exactly talk about it, but one day we snuck back to the cabin after lunch, and he was going down on me when this older kid came in. He wasn't a counselor, just some sixteen-year-old douchebag from another cabin. He got really nasty, called us all kinds of names."

Nate bit his tongue, hoping he wasn't going to end up bleeding before Kellan finished his story.

"We were scared shitless, I mean, it's not like there was

another explanation for us both with our shorts off and David's head in my lap. If I'd been thinking, maybe I could have turned it on him, like he wasn't where he was supposed to be either. But the guy said he'd tell everyone. And the counselors would call our parents."

As the direction the story was going got pretty obvious, Nate felt sick. He stopped stroking Kellan's hair, shifting to hold his face, to stop his story with a kiss, but Kellan cut Nate's motion off with a look.

"He said he'd keep his mouth shut if we did it for him—gave him a blowjob. David said he'd do it, that I wouldn't have to, but the guy said it had to be both of us. Told us to meet him in the bathroom that night or he'd tell."

Did you want a My First Blowjob *T-shirt?* The memory of Nate's words burned in his throat like bile. *I want to be here, Nate. Whatever it costs.* Nate had taken Kellan's offer and used his mouth rather than letting him find his own way.

Nate had to make himself keep listening, keep looking at Kellan.

"It wasn't too bad. He couldn't get off with it, had to jerk himself off the rest of the way." But Kellan's mouth pulled into a grimace as if he was reliving it. "But goddamn that pissed me off."

And what had Nate done that first night? Demanded Kellan suck him off to prove how desperate he was for a place to stay. Exactly how different was he from this asshole who'd raped a couple younger kids? Kellan should have bitten it off.

"It wasn't too bad," Kellan said again. "But David was pretty freaked out. He ended up going home three weeks early. I wanted to kill that prick every time I saw him. But it kind of made me mad at you too, and I know that was stupid. Like if you'd been there—I don't know. But when we got to high school and the older kids started saying stuff about you—I couldn't be on that other side again. I was a fucking coward, but I couldn't do it."

"No. You weren't a coward." But Nate was because he couldn't look at him now with the knowledge of how he'd acted hanging there between them. "That was rape."

"Oh, c'mon. He barely did anything."

"So abuse or harassment, whatever. Fuck." Nate pushed up, swung his legs over the side of the bed, sat up and squeezed the back of his neck. "It's no different from the shit I pulled when you came here looking for help."

"Huh?"

"I don't know how you can stand to be in the same room with me."

Kellan might forgive him, but Nate would never be able to forgive himself.

"That?" Kellan sat next to him. "You were—we were messing around. Nothing happened."

Christ. The way he'd let Nate fuck his mouth, the way Kellan had opened, yielded, turned all sweet and submissive— where did it come from? It wasn't real. Right when Kellan had been figuring out sex, some bastard abused him and fucked with his head.

"You wouldn't say that if you weren't in denial. You should have had therapy."

"Don't." Kellan slammed a fist onto his own thigh. "Don't you dare fucking turn this into one of those letters for your fucking column."

Nate couldn't be having this conversation naked, with a used condom next to his hand, not when he'd screwed up this badly. He dragged himself free of the bed he'd have sworn he wouldn't be getting out of before morning—or a lot more orgasms.

"Yeah, standard Hey Gray's advice. Run."

"For Christsake, I'm just putting some clothes on."

"Yeah, sex over, back to business. You know it's kind of funny. I'm not the one who has a problem with his sexuality, man. You are."

"That's bullshit. I've known since I was thirteen. Younger." The slithering sensation in Nate's stomach was from having come that hard, not from any guilt about being gay.

"You might have known, but you wish you didn't. You're the one who's got issues about wanting to fuck guys. I don't."

"You don't know what you're saying." Nate yanked his briefs up. He grabbed the first T-shirt he found, and it dropped below his hips. Kellan's, damn it.

Kellan sprawled on the edge of the bed, legs wide, and leaned back on his hands. He winced and sat up straight.

Nate ripped Kellan's shirt off and stood in front of him. How could Kellan think that? Just because Nate didn't get mushy over a fuck didn't mean he had some kind of hang-up about sex. "You're wrong. I don't have any issue with wanting to pound your tight ass again."

Kellan caught the shirt with his left hand. "Even with my history of abuse?"

Nate's cheeks heated, an unfamiliar blush. He was fine with being gay. There was nothing wrong with being gay. It was nothing to be ashamed of.

Kellan pushed out his lower lip. "That's right. Who kept telling me I wasn't ready? Like having sex with someone I...care about was some prize I had to suffer and prove myself for."

Nate turned away. "I never said it was. I'm fine with who I

am."

"That lie is so big I can't believe it didn't choke you." Kellan yanked the shirt over his head, stood up and winced again, though whether that was about his hand or his ass Nate couldn't tell. Kellan stuffed a pair of clean briefs in a pocket and dragged on the jeans Nate had pulled off last night. "Because really, you're just a scared little shit who can't see past his little boxes of good guys and bad guys. I'm not going to wait around for you to find a way to turn your freakout into a reason to run from me."

This was insane. Nate didn't have a problem with being gay. And he wanted Kellan here. Maybe they could shove all this stuff from the past under the repression carpet and everything would be fine again.

"You don't have to leave."

"Yeah. I do. Right now." Kellan picked up his wallet from the bowl near the door. "See ya around."

Nate was tired of swallowing all the anger, all the frustration. "Right. Because when you don't get the kind of attention you like, you throw a fucking tantrum." Something crashed near his desk as Yin dove for cover. Nate had no idea his voice could get that loud.

"I told you something about me. Something I never told anyone, and you turned it into some big issue for *you*. Check your own fucking tantrum, Nate."

"I can see why your father got tired of all your drama. What are you going to try next? Becoming a Rastafarian?"

Kellan threw his keys across the room to skitter under the bed, and Yin streaked into the bathroom.

Nate had control of himself again. "Stop scaring my cat."

Kellan loomed over him, and Christ, he was beautiful and

he smelled so good with sex and sweat still clinging to him. Nate wasn't scared. He couldn't help it if Kellan couldn't handle the truth about his behavior.

"Do you have any idea what I gave up for you?" Kellan's cheeks were dark red, green eyes bright.

"Yeah, five million dollars. Like you'd let me forget that."

"I'm not talking about the money. I gave up everything. Everything I thought I understood about myself, about my life, because—" Kellan's throat worked.

How could Nate have only had the right to touch him—kiss him—for such a short time?

"You're the best thing I've ever had in my life," Kellan said.

Now Nate was scared. It was too much. Too much responsibility. This wasn't a faceless person emailing Hey Gray, this was—the most important person in his life. How could Nate make him happy when he couldn't seem to do that for himself? And it wasn't about being gay, damn it.

"It's easy to be confused when I'm all you have. I don't want you to wake up and realize that this—especially the sex—was because you didn't have any other option." Nate said it softly, the anger safely locked away again, but Kellan took a step back as if Nate had shoved him.

"The only thing I'm likely to do is wake up and realize that you're pathetic. You really should learn to get over yourself before even your cat can't fit in the room with your self-righteous gay halo."

Kellan left.

Chapter Twenty-Two

On Sunday, Nate was in his office alternating between writing his next column and writing a letter that magically explained everything and made Kellan happy and living in Nate's studio on Castle Street again. It had only been one night. Kellan was right. Nate was pathetic. He'd made it fifteen years without Kellan Brooks taking up a huge space in his world, he could make it again.

Besides, Nate knew he was right. It was only a matter of time before Kellan realized he couldn't give up D-cups or actresses forever. Not that Nate had asked him to.

Eli walked in without knocking.

Nate saved his column and buried his scribbles under ad copy on his desk. "You're not working today."

"Thanks for the update. Here's one for you. Your boyfriend spent the night on my over-crowded apartment's couch, if you care."

So Kellan hadn't gone crawling back to Geoffrey's money. Good for him. But where did Eli get off blaming Nate?

"And for your information, I didn't kick him out. He left."

Eli sat on a pile of folders. Nate's office was perfectly organized. He kept the folders there so no one would come in and sit down.

"I'm sure it was still your fault." Eli put his arms on the desk and leaned in, studying Nate's face. "Do you like being unhappy, is that it?"

"I'm not unhappy."

Eli shrugged. "So you're just a dick."

"Yes. And right now I'm the dick who's telling you to get out of my office so I can get my work done."

"Fine, Boss." Eli stood and headed for the door.

"And tell Kellan he's welcome to come back. I'll pick up an air mattress for him."

Eli stopped and turned back to Nate's desk. "Nate, if you guys were faking it all that time, why is now the first time you think of an air mattress?"

"Well, I'm not sure if the cat—"

"It's really thick vinyl, and Yin isn't a destructive cat. Face it. You've always been in love with him."

Nate had faced that a long time ago. "Sorry to ruin your dreams of true love, but that doesn't change anything when that isn't the problem."

"No. Because you're the problem. Sucks to be you, Boss. And not in the good way." Eli left.

Nate was gathering up some great exit lines if he ever wanted to do a Queertiquette column on them.

He lifted his notes out from under the ad. He wasn't unhappy. He wasn't happy. The world full of people deliberately screwing over other people, and Nate was only trying to fix a little bit of it.

If he'd told Kellan that—not about the world, but about loving him—maybe that would have kept him there. Maybe it would be enough to bring him back.

Nate's direct line rang. "Gray."

"Hey, Gray." Kellan's voice had a light mocking tone to it, one that made Nate's stomach turn over in a way he remembered too well from high school.

"What?"

"That's a nice way to say hello to the guy you fucked yesterday. Have you ever had a relationship that got past the first fuck—I mean besides your first one, Malcolm? He must have been some kind of saint to deserve you."

"Kellan, I'm at work."

"I know. I'm the one who dialed the number. This is all about business, Mr. Gray."

"What is?"

"If I make a deal, I stick to it. Tomorrow I'll take you to my dad's office and get you the stuff you need to fuck over Geoffrey's plans to screw the city out of millions."

"And how are you going to do that?"

"The same way I always was. Wear a suit and tie and meet me at Eli's at eleven tomorrow. Find some way to cover the stitches, and bring a briefcase if you've got one."

Nate had one. His parents had given him a beautiful case when he graduated from college. A year early.

"Be on time. And look nervous," Kellan said before he hung up.

That wouldn't be a problem.

Casey, one of Eli's roommates, had a car, and she gave them a lift to Dundalk as Kellan went over his plan. He had on a pair of black jeans Nate had never seen and a new shirt.

"Every year my dad's secretary takes a vacation in May.

She's completely unreachable and my dad drives every secretary they send in crazy. They don't want to be there subbing for her, and he doesn't want to deal with them. Every Monday he has this lunch where his leaders report in. He'll be gone for about two hours. Geoffrey won't have said anything to the substitute secretary about me, so we can get in the office no trouble. You just do what I say."

Nate wiped his sweaty hands on his suit pants. This was definitely illegal. And maybe still immoral, even if they did stop Geoffrey Brooks from devastating the city's tax base. It didn't seem to matter anymore. Nate had helped Kellan because that was what Nate wanted to do. He'd wanted Kellan Brooks as a boyfriend since learning what the word meant and had grabbed whatever rationalization would make it work.

So why was Nate in this car, wearing a suit and tie, briefcase on the backseat next to him? Kellan turned, looking over the front seat as they got to the industrial section. Nate wished he could blame this stunt on responding to the challenge in Kellan's eyes, but it wasn't about proving himself, like when Kellan would dare him when they were kids. Nate was here because he wanted to be. Because Kellan was, and in his suit jacket's inside pocket were Nate's notes about all those things he was trying to figure out how to explain.

"Go around to the other side. You can drop us off in the back." Kellan pointed. The parking lot was gated, but there was no attendant in the little booth in front. Casey pulled around one end of the building and stopped where Kellan indicated a gray fire door.

"The smokers always leave this door open during the day," Kellan said as they got out. True enough, there was a newspaper—last week's *Charming Rag*, actually—holding the door open a crack. They stepped into the bottom of a stairwell. "I'd tell you to remember to look nervous, but I think you've got that covered."

"Kellan, maybe—"

Kellan swung around to face him. "Afraid? Don't you want your payback for what he did to your family?"

"I don't know."

"Liar."

Kellan led the way upstairs, then down a hall and through doors, and finally stopped in front of a secretary's post with a wide custom-shaped desk in Brooks Blasts' gold-flecked crimson.

"Hey, Amanda, right? Tina's out?"

The woman looked about the age of Nate's mom, and she did have a harried look as she eyed the blinking phone and a stack of papers and her computer screen.

"Vacation."

"Right. That most dreaded time of the year, when Dad gets even crankier than usual."

Damn, Kellan was good. She was already smiling. It was like he was a hypnotist.

"You meet Nate, yet? He's a new guy in marketing."

Amanda shook her head, and Nate gave her an entirely unfeigned nervous wave.

"Dad had me go to lunch with him today, and evidently there's something they've got to have and Nate's the one who has to come get it. You know how Dad is when Tina's not here to make sure he's got everything he needs."

Amanda flicked a sympathetic gaze in Nate's direction, then held up a finger as she answered the phone. Nate hoped like hell it wasn't Geoffrey.

"I'm sorry, he's in a meeting. Can I take a message for you?

Oh, Mrs. Brooks, I'm so sorry."

Kellan grinned and held out a hand for the phone.

"But Kellan's here." Amanda handed off the phone.

"Hi, Mom. Thanks for the clothes... Yes, I'm going to talk to him." Kellan looked at Amanda and signaled for her keys. "That's up to him... Yeah, Mom, I know."

The panic making the blood pound in Nate's ears eased back. Kellan wasn't completely cut off if his mother was helping him. Nate knew she would. And maybe they would pull this off without getting arrested.

Kellan passed back the phone, and Amanda handed over a set of keys.

Geoffrey Brooks's office didn't look any different from any other businessman's where Nate had conducted interviews. Heavy furniture designed to impress, an inspirational eagle print on one wall, framed citations and photos over the credenza. But after everything that had happened, Nate felt like he was tiptoeing on sleeping alligators.

Kellan went right over to the desk. "This is where he keeps the good stuff. Like his security code isn't obvious. It's the last four digits of Keegan's social security number and the date they got the news. Dad still carries his dog tag."

A mechanical whir sounded, and Kellan pulled open a file drawer. "Here." He started putting files on the desk. "You've got a camera phone, right?"

"Yeah." Nate really didn't want to look in those files.

"C'mon. We don't have all day."

Nate flipped open the first one and snapped a picture of each page of the official proposal, before finding the real plans in the next file. Standard shell game. The company was buying the abandoned plant, but they wouldn't be employing more than fifty people. Only a high-end staff of research and development like Nate's dad had done for KZ Cola, nothing to justify the job-creation tax breaks Geoffrey was looking for.

"Nate." Kellan's voice was a little weird. "Is this that formula? The patent thing?" He handed Nate a file.

Nate didn't have much of a chemistry background, but he knew what his father had worked on. He'd managed some ethyl bonding to get a better flavor result with fewer parts per million with heliotropin, the stuff that made the company's cream soda taste so good. But although Nate's dad had been the one to do all the work, the company got all the credit, so he came up with another one at home.

According to his dad, he'd managed not only to get a creamier feel with the new bonds, but improved the aroma factor of the heliotropin to make people drinking it have enhanced good moods.

Nate knew enough to read that it was the chemical structure his dad had worked on, had seen the molecular diagrams enough in the house. The buzzing in his ears was back, but from pure excitement. This was better proof than anything about the plans for the plant. He could take this back to his dad, they could prove that the former junior marketing executive had stolen his friend's work and built a billion-dollar corporation out of it.

"Is it?" Kellan asked.

"Yeah. It's my dad's."

"So why is my dad's name on the patent?" Kellan pointed over Nate's shoulder.

"Because he fucking stole it."

"And why didn't your dad come after him?"

"Wait." Nate turned through a couple of pages clipped in

the file under the patent. "It's an affidavit, signed by my dad. It swears that he had nothing to do with the creation of Compound E and that all rights are assigned to Geoffrey Brooks as its sole inventor."

"My dad can barely mix whiskey and soda."

Nate looked back at the molecule, the description of the compound. "My dad was so pissed at KZ Cola for taking all the credit for that first thing he made." The realization made his legs feel like buttered noodles, and he had to put his hand on the desk. "He took it and changed it just enough."

"And gave it to my dad? Why?" Kellan had moved so close Nate could feel the heat from his body, the solid strength of him there.

"Because KZ came after him. And my dad didn't care about anything but getting back at KZ, so he gave it to your dad."

"So why didn't my dad help yours when he lost his job?"

"Because the lawyers and accountants at KZ would have used that to bankrupt us both," said a voice behind them.

Nate jumped, landing against Kellan, who put a hand on his arm to steady him.

Geoffrey Brooks closed his office door behind him. Nate would have known Kellan's dad anywhere, tall and broad like his son, with blond hair turned a snowy white.

"And your father would have gone to jail," Mr. Brooks continued as he walked behind his desk. "Like someone might for breaking and entering, Nathan." He swept the files into a pile and held out his hand for the one Nate still clutched.

Nate closed it and passed it back.

"If anyone's going to jail, it's me." Kellan faced his father. "I'm the one who broke in here."

"No, you managed to convince Amanda to give you her

keys. If you put half your talents toward something useful—"

"Because helping out other people the way he does isn't useful?" Nate couldn't believe he'd dared to interrupt Mr. Brooks.

The way Mr. Brooks looked at him made Nate's skin itch, but he stood his ground.

"My son and I will discuss that later. Right now, Nathan, you will excuse yourself and consider yourself lucky I don't press charges."

"I have something to say first."

Unlike his son's green, Mr. Brooks's eyes were a pale blue, piercing. "I doubt I want to hear it."

"I owe you an apology, sir. What my father did was wrong, and based on my own conclusions I have given you and your company unfair scrutiny in the paper." He'd never lied about anything he'd printed, but since his column was opinion, there was a little leeway in his inferences.

Mr. Brooks's sandy brows arched high. "Unfair scrutiny?"

"If you want me to write a retraction, I will."

"What I want is to sever any association with you, and for you to sever any with my son."

"That's not happening, Dad."

"If you will excuse us, Nathan?"

"No. If he's not good enough to be in your presence, neither am I." Kellan hadn't moved, still so close that if Nate had been in his usual T-shirt, the hair standing on end on his arms would have reached to Kellan's sleeve.

"He was good enough to land you in the hospital, I see." Mr. Brooks nodded at the splint on Kellan's finger, the ace bandage around his wrist.

"No, a bunch of bigots like you did that."

"That's what I'm trying to tell you. Both of you. Nathan, you were a bright boy, look at the world and tell me that this is something a father wants for his son."

Nate's father had never made him think being gay was something wrong, but he'd never said he was proud of him either. He'd always been wrapped up in the bitter unfairness of his life.

"I don't know. I'm not a father."

"And you never will be. At least understand that. Kellan, what have I built this for if not for your children?"

"Being gay doesn't mean you can't have kids," Kellan said.

"And what kind of life is that for them? To be picked on? To learn that the people they think are their parents are unnatural? Why would anyone do that to a child?"

"Why would anyone tell his son he wished he'd never been born?" Nate felt that anger rising in him again, and this time he wasn't afraid of it.

"Get out of my office."

"Fine." Kellan grabbed Nate's hand.

"Kellan." Geoffrey Brooks's voice snapped through the air like a live current, crackling against Nate's skin. He gripped Kellan's hand. "Did you know your little bandwagon is funded by grants? I'm sure there are others in the community who would feel uncomfortable about a homosexual having access to all those helpless people. It wouldn't take much to cut that funding."

Nate could feel Kellan shrink at his father's words. He'd already given up one job because of this asshole, he wasn't losing another, not one he loved.

"You would seriously penalize those same helpless people in rehab centers because you can't make your adult son do what you want him to do? If you think the paper has been hard on you before, wait until they see this."

"I'll have you arrested for burglary."

A tremor went through Kellan's hands.

"Great. More publicity. That way everyone in Baltimore, hell, everyone in the country's going to want to read about the man who took therapy away from brain-damaged kids because he didn't like who his son was dating." After giving a reassuring squeeze, Nate held his hands, wrists up, toward Brooks. "Did you call security yet? Can you wait until I get a camera down here?"

Anger was good. Nate had never felt better in his life. And he wasn't out of control.

"Don't forget to arrest me too, Dad. I'm the one who let him in." Kellan held up his wrists.

"Your type has a penchant for drama." Brooks folded his arms and sighed.

"My type has a penchant for spending their considerable disposable income on products from companies that don't engage in homophobic practices. You might want to think about that on your profit-and-loss sheets, Mr. Brooks."

"Fine. If anything happens to the funding for the recreation program, I won't be responsible. Can I assume the same discretion about these proprietary documents?" Brooks put his hand on the files.

"No," Kellan said. "You can't screw with people like that."

And yesterday Nate would have said the same thing. There was a right and a wrong, and damn anyone who tried to stop him from pointing that out. He'd built his whole life on justifying his father's integrity, with Geoffrey Brooks as his personal bogeyman. That was all as stable as a sandcastle in a hurricane. His father had wasted his life on petty revenge, and Geoffrey Brooks was only another closed-minded bigot.

Nate had done enough for the greater good. Now he was going to look out for something a little closer to home. Kellan.

"It would take a lot more than you not pulling that grant to sit on a story like this." Nate smiled. "Kellan shouldn't have to keep wondering what your next threat will be."

Brooks appealed to his son. "Kellan, after what happened to your brother—don't you see I'm only trying to protect you?"

"Then let me be a man, Dad. My own man."

Chapter Twenty-Three

Kellan thought Amanda might be risking her job when she offered to have Shep drop them off somewhere, and he'd probably gotten her in enough trouble already, so he shook his head and hurried to catch up to Nate who was striding down the hall toward the back stairs.

Kellan punched the elevator button. "This way is closer to the street."

"The sooner I get out of here the better." Nate and his fucking principles and a long-ass walk for no good reason. Of course, Nate and his fucking principles had just made hash out of Kellan's dad, so instead of telling Nate to meet him out front, Kellan jogged down the hall after him. Damn, Nate could walk fast when he was pissed.

Nate didn't say a word, even after they'd cleared the smokers' door and started through the parking lot.

"You were kick ass, man. Thanks for having my back."

Nate stopped, glanced at Kellan and then started walking more slowly. "You had mine."

"Hell of a team."

Nate led them toward Dundalk Ave. Squinting, Kellan could barely see the bus shelter way down the street.

As they waited at a light, Nate touched his arm. Kellan

looked down into eyes so focused and intense he wanted to shiver, because he knew what it was like when Nate turned that loose. Had seen all of him. Loved all of him. Sexy, loyal, angry, funny, and as irritating as that fucking self-righteousness was, Kellan loved that too, because without it, he'd never have had any of this. Not standing up to his dad, or teaching Marisol to sing as a way of talking to her family, or finding out that having Nate's dick up his ass was guaranteed to make Kellan come harder than he ever thought he could.

He wanted to kiss him, but even he knew that the industrial part of Dundalk was not exactly the place for an outburst of affection.

Nate offered a half smile that didn't touch the heat in his eyes. "No matter what happened, we're still friends, right?"

"The 'what happened' being sex, right?"

"Yeah." Nate shifted his case around as he shrugged out of his suit jacket. "I—I was kind of a dick. I should have been a— more supportive listener when you told me about what happened."

"A more supportive listener?"

Nate trying to dig himself out of this hole and falling in deeper was kind of funny, and the fact that Kellan wanted to laugh Nate out of his wounded dignity more than listen to the apology Nate owed him was proof of exactly how stupidly in love Kellan was with the guy.

"A better friend." Nate looked off into the distance like the bus would spare him having to get through this. "You were right. I'm not really good at being friends with people. I tend to get on their nerves. But, there's one thing I'm good at and that's learning how to make something work better."

"That's a lot of words, Nate. What are you saying?"

"Can we still be— Christ, I don't mean it like that." Nate

squeezed the back of his head. "I want you to stay part of my life."

"Well, Eli seems to put up with you all right. Despite your best efforts to shake him loose."

"He's too young to know better."

Kellan let the laugh slip out. "Yeah. I think we can still be friends."

"Thanks."

The sun shimmered off the bus, making it ripple as it rolled toward them.

"Your mom's helping you out?"

"Well, she wired me enough cash to buy some decent clothes. God, getting money that way is fucking complicated."

"Yeah." Now that Nate had finished his speech he didn't seem to know what to say.

"So how far back up does this bus go?"

"Up to Johns Hopkins Bayview. Um, where are you headed?"

"I thought I'd go in to see how Marisol is doing. I can't play the guitar, but I can still work with her. I'll check in with Jeff."

"Right. You know, you're still welcome to stay—I could get an air mattress or a futon or something."

Kellan wanted to take pity on him, but this earnest, trying-too-fucking-hard Nate was too much fun. He deserved a little payback.

The bus's air brakes made a nasal blast as it jolted to a stop in front of them.

"Meet me after work and we'll talk about it."

"Where?"

Kellan pretended to think a minute. "J.J.'s."

Being late made Nate physically sick. Being late today, wondering if Kellan would still be there waiting while Nate was stuck at the *Rag's* offices in a forty-five minute phone call to placate a major advertiser over a double-booked back cover infected him like a full-body toothache. He dry swallowed Tylenol and swore that the marketing director and the graphics editor were never allowed to be out on the same day again, no matter who the Orioles were playing or what their record was. He'd rather be back covering local bands and their tragically over-hip groupies than running the office.

At least by six, traffic flow had gotten light enough that he was able to push the scooter as fast as it would go as he headed north.

He parked it in the same alley and hit the door. Kellan was sitting at the bar in the same spot Nate had occupied six weeks ago. Scooter in the same alley, Kellan in the same spot. After work on a Monday. Nate wasn't slow.

"Hey." He walked up and nudged Kellan with his shoulder.

Kellan looked at him and took a long swallow from his bottle.

"I hear you're gay now."

"I'm in a gay bar," Kellan pointed out with a shrug.

"Good, because I need a boyfriend."

"Blow me."

"Anytime, anywhere, baby."

"I don't know. I might need a boyfriend who isn't such a control freak."

Nate leaned close to his ear. "You want to fuck my ass, Kell? Then let's get out of here."

Kellan coughed on his beer. "Okay. I was just—I mean, you don't have to—"

"No, but you do."

Kellan started to wipe his mouth with his sore hand and then switched. He licked his lips and Nate kissed them, using his tongue to invite Kellan's to follow him back. Kellan grabbed Nate's head and held it. The ache faded from his body, melting into the wooden floor. Kellan was better than all the damned Tylenol in the world.

Kellan lifted his head. "I'm good with things the way they are."

Nate ran his tongue over Kellan's jaw, right below his ear. "Why do you think I have a dildo in the drawer next to my bed?"

Kellan jumped off the barstool and slapped a ten on the bar. Nate swore he was about to push the scooter—or the truck blocking them—when they went down Washington. But when they got in the apartment, Kellan seemed to run out of steam.

Nate steered him toward the couch, stripping them both. He looked at the tie in his hands and then at Kellan, sprawled on the couch, bandaged hand over his head. Another time.

Yeah, suddenly they had all the time and the laters in the world. Nate's heart did that clichéd beat skip again, and he swallowed hard as he fished supplies out of the drawer. Swallowing didn't loosen his chest. Religion might be the opiate of the masses, but sometimes confession was good for the soul.

He went to his knees in front of Kellan. "I love you, you know that? Always fucking have."

Kellan brushed his thumb across Nate's lips, smoothing his beard. "Yeah. I do."

Nate caught Kellan's hand and kissed his palm, then rubbed his face in it.

Kellan's fingers curled as if it tickled.

"I could shave it if you want—if it's too weird."

"It's you."

Nate didn't tease or lick, he went at Kellan's dick and swallowed it, gulped him in until his pubes tickled Nate's lips before slowly backing off.

"Holy shit," Kellan breathed, and put his hand softly on Nate's head.

Nate pulled off all the way and lined them up, urging Kellan's hand to hold him tighter. He hesitated for a second. Control was an illusion. He'd never had any where Kellan was concerned. "Like this, baby. Fuck my face."

Kellan shuddered and pushed in. Nate could tell the instant Kellan got over worrying about Nate's breathing and gave into the feel of Nate's mouth and tongue and throat.

"Fucking killing me," Kellan gasped.

Nate let Kellan have it for awhile, until he felt the tightening of the skin over his lips, the tremors in Kellan's thighs.

He wrenched his head free. "Wait, baby."

Kellan's eyes were hooded under his long bangs as he watched Nate grab the lube to pump some onto his fingers. "Are you gonna?"

Nate reached behind himself and slicked his hole. He squirted a little into Kellan's hand. "Put it on the head of your dick."

Kellan gave his dick a lazy swipe as Nate tore the condom open with his teeth.

Kellan took it from him before he could roll it down. "I'd better do it."

Once the rubber was on, they both ran their lube-covered hands over it.

Before Kellan could stop and think again, Nate pushed him back against the couch and straddled him on a foot and one knee. Kellan put a hand on Nate's hip and a tremor ran through them both. Sometimes sex was just sex, he'd given that advice often enough, and sometimes it was a whole hell of a lot more.

Reaching back, he guided Kellan's cock into place and sank down enough to feel the stretch.

Kellan grabbed Nate's ass with both hands, the splint jabbing into Nate's glutes.

"Easy. Gimme a second." Nate closed his eyes and finally managed to take the head, then slid slowly down the shaft.

"Nate."

He opened his eyes.

"Yeah." Kellan held his gaze.

Nate started riding him, but Kellan kept trying to go deeper, desperation spilling into a whine in his throat. Nate worked himself faster, holding onto the couch and Kellan's shoulder for support.

"Fuck, that's tight and I need, Nate, I need to—" Kellan bucked up.

"Yeah, I got you."

With a wince, Nate pulled off and put his knee on the couch next to Kellan. Gripping the back of the frame, Nate stuck his ass up and tipped his head at Kellan.

Kellan scrambled eagerly off the couch, and Nate turned his head away to hide a deep breath. He liked the pressure of a cock in his ass, but he didn't bottom like this. Except he did now. Because the look on Kellan's face was worth fighting with himself to let go, to let Kellan take over.

Kellan wrapped an arm around him and slammed inside, too much too fast, and Nate groaned.

"Sorry."

"Don't be sorry. But you'd better make sure I get off before you come."

"Control freak."

Nate wrapped a tight fist around his dick as Kellan started to fuck him. One shift of their hips, and Kellan had the perfect angle. Fucking beginner's luck. Nate wanted to tease him with it, but he couldn't do much but groan with the thick pressure rubbing across his gland, body crowded full of Kellan, in him and on him and around him. A heavy breath in Nate's ear, the snap of balls against his ass as Kellan drove him into the couch again and again.

The last thought Nate had before he just gave in to what Kellan was doing to his body was a pang of regret at not putting a towel on the cushion. Then Kellan started moving in quick jabs that brought Nate right up under the edge. Tightening his ass muscles to help them both along, he worked his cock and let it go, let it flood through him and pour out of him, trusting Kellan to keep them both upright as Nate's body locked out everything but the bursts of pleasure flying from his dick.

Kellan grunted and took two deep strokes before he was coming too, shaking and gasping against Nate's skin, leaving the imprint of Kellan all over him.

Nate buried a wince in his forearms as Kellan pulled out.

"So, do I need an air mattress?" Yeah, Nate might be willing to put his ass and his pride on the line for Kellan, but damned if he'd let him get the last word.

"You need a real bed. We need a real apartment."

"We?"

"Me and Yin. You can come live there too, but some of us are carnivores."

"Okay."

Kellan dragged Nate onto the couch where they got tangled up and stickier. "You're kind of easy after getting fucked. I'm going to remember that."

"Don't get too used to it."

"How about every time you piss me off?"

"Define pissed off." Nate lifted his head so he could see Kellan's face.

"Contemplating exactly how much five million could buy."

"Okay."

"One more thing." Kellan was grinning. "As much fun as this stuff is—"

"'This stuff' meaning sex?"

"Yes. As much fun as fucking our brains out is, we're getting a TV. At least thirty-six inches. And satellite. And—"

Nate stopped him with a kiss. "What happens when I get pissed off?"

"I'll piss you off more until you fuck me stupid."

About the Author

K.A. Mitchell discovered the magic of writing at an early age when she learned that a carefully crayoned note of apology sent to the kitchen in a toy truck would earn her a reprieve from banishment to her room. Her career as a spin control artist was cut short when her family moved to a two-story house, and her trucks would not roll safely down the stairs. Around the same time, she decided that Chip and Ken made a much cuter couple than Ken and Barbie and was perplexed when invitations to play Barbie dropped off. An unnamed number of years later, she's happy to find other readers and writers who like to play in her world.

To learn more about K.A. Mitchell, please visit www.kamitchell.com. Send an email to K.A. Mitchell at authorKAMitchell@gmail.com.

Can love repair a shattered life in time to save the world?

The Salisbury Key
© 2011 Harper Fox

Daniel Logan is on a lonely quest to find out what drove his lover, a wealthy, respected archaeologist, to take his own life. The answer—the elusive "key" for which Jason was desperately searching—lies somewhere on a dangerous and deadly section of Salisbury Plain.

The only way to gain access, though, is to allow an army explosives expert to help him navigate the bomb-riddled military zone. A man he met once more than three years ago, who is even more serious and enigmatic than before.

Lieutenant Rayne has better things to do than risk his life protecting a scientist on an apparent suicide mission. Like get back to Iraq and prove he will never again miss another roadside bomb. Yet as he helps Dan uncover the truth, an attraction neither man is in the mood for springs up against their will. And stirs up the nervous attention of powerfully placed people—military and academic alike.

First in conflict, then in passion, Rayne and Dan are drawn together in a relationship as rocky and complicated as the ancient land they search. Where every step leads them closer to a terrible legacy written in death...

Warning: Contains bombs, archaeology and explicit M/M sex, not necessarily in that order.

Available now in ebook and print from Samhain Publishing.

Love was never part of his plan...until it pounced.

With Abandon
© 2011 J.L. Langley

As heir to an old and proud heritage, Aubrey Reynolds works and lives for his family, his employees and his pack. Agreeing to watch after a visiting werewolf is no big deal—until he discovers the newcomer is his mate. His very *male* mate...which is a very big deal, indeed. Revealing his sexuality was never part of Aubrey's well-ordered life plan.

Much as he loved caring for his eight younger brothers, Matt Mahihkan knows it's time to grab the opportunity to attend college in Atlanta. Realizing Aubrey is his mate should have been a delightful experience...except Aubrey treats him more like a dirty little secret than a lover. Yet Matt is a patient man. Aubrey can't stay in the closet forever. Can he?

In time, they settle into a comfortable, if complicated, routine. Until a rogue werewolf with an axe to grind forces Aubrey to add to the wedge of secrets driving him and Matt apart, leaving Matt exposed to danger...and Aubrey forced to choose between love and duty.

Warning: Contains color abuse with a really bad sense of fashion, a southern accent from hell, sex on antique furniture, a pouncing playful werewolf, obnoxious siblings, liberal use of a color identifier and impatient sex. No lightning bugs were harmed in the making of this book.

Available now in ebook and print from Samhain Publishing.

www.samhainpublishing.com

Green for the planet.
Great for your wallet.

SAMHAIN
PUBLISHING

It's all about the story...

Romance

HORROR

Retro
ROMANCE

www.samhainpublishing.com

CPSIA information can be obtained at www.ICGtesting.com
Printed in the USA
BVOW041357260412

288764BV00001B/56/P